"Okay, so here's the way I see it," Heather said. "We're here for our last real vacation before we head to college, which will be very serious and boring and not fun."

"It will? What about the parties?" I asked. "The football games, the frats—our glory days?"

"Just work with me for a second. What I'm trying to say is that we have fourteen days here, so let's find some amazing guys to have summer flings with. Are you in?"

"Uh . . . is that the plan?" I asked. She made it sound so easy.

"Pretty much. I'll help you find a guy, and you'll help me find one, which shouldn't be that hard because it seems like there are tons of them around here on vacation just like us. . . ."

"True," I agreed, thinking of our hot next-door neighbor, whatever his name was.

ALSO BY CATHERINE CLARK:

CATHERINE CLARK

Picture Perfect

HARPER TEEN

An Imprint of HarperCollinsPublishers

HarperTeen is an imprint
of HarperCollins Publishers.

Picture Perfect
Copyright © 2008 by Catherine Clark
All rights reserved. Printed in the United States of America.
No part of this book may be used or reproduced in any manner what-
soever without written permission except in the case of brief quota-
tions embodied in critical articles and reviews. For information
address HarperCollins Children's Books, a division of HarperCollins
Publishers, 1350 Avenue of the Americas, New York, NY 10019.
www.harperteen.com

Library of Congress catalog card number: 2007930289
ISBN 978-0-06-137497-5

Typography by Andrea Vandergrift
❖
First Edition

Picture
Perfect

Chapter 1

"*I* can't *wait* to see all the guys."

You might have thought that was me talking, as I headed into the town of Kill Devil Hills, North Carolina, my destination for a two-week summer stay on the Outer Banks.

But no. It was my dad, of all people.

And it's not what you might be thinking *now*, either. He was talking about seeing his best friends from college.

We meet up every few years on a big reunion trip with "the guys," their wives, their kids, and other assorted members of their families—dogs, parents, random cousins, nannies, you name it. I think it's Dad's favorite vacation, because he and his buddies play golf, sit around

1

reminiscing, and stay up late talking every night.

Even though that occasionally gets a little boring, I like going on these trips, because I've gotten to be friends with "the guys'" offspring, who have sprung off like me: Heather Olsen, Adam Thompson, and Spencer Flanagan. I couldn't wait to see all of them. It had been two years since the last vacation reunion for the four of us, which was *almost*, but not quite, long enough to make me forget what an idiot I'd made of myself the last time, when I was fifteen, Spencer was sixteen, and I'd told him that I thought he was really cool and that we really clicked and that I wished we lived closer because then we could . . . well, you get the gist. *Embarrassing*. With a capital *E*. Maybe three of them, in fact. EEEmbarrassing. Like an extra-wide foot that I'd stuck in my mouth.

But enough about me and my slipup. I basically love these trips because we end up in cool locations like this, a place I'd never seen, or even gotten close to seeing, before now.

Living in the Midwest, we don't get to the

coast much. And this was even beyond the coast—if that's possible—on a strip of land that was as far as you could get without becoming an island. Or maybe it was an island. What do I know? We live in "fly-over land." On the plus side, we don't have earthquakes, hurricanes, or tropical storms. On the minus side, we have the occasional nearby tornado and no ocean access.

"This is just *beautiful*," Mom said as we turned off the main four-lane road, and onto a smaller road with giant three- and four-story beach houses on each side of it. "Isn't it, Emily?"

"Those houses are gigantic. Is that where we're staying? In one of those?" I asked.

"Yup. Remember the pictures we checked out online?" Dad asked from the front seat of our rental car. We'd flown into Norfolk, Virginia, and driven south from there.

"Not really," I said. I hadn't paid all that much attention, to be honest. I was too busy finishing up my senior year, getting my college plans set, figuring out how to squeeze a two-week vacation into a summer in which I needed to make as much money as possible.

In July and August, I'd be back home working at Constant Camera full-time, saving money for textbooks and anything else I might need when I got to college. Fortunately, I'd received a few gifts for my graduation that would help out a lot—gift cards, as well as supplies for my hopefully budding career in photography. I planned to take lots of pictures while on this vacation, and turn them into something I could give everyone at the end of the two weeks—a calendar. I'd left my new Mac at home because of the hassle of traveling with it—Mom was afraid it would get I-Jacked—and I'd brought my inexpensive camera instead of my digital SLR, so I wasn't working with my usual stuff. But I was still confident I could get plenty of good pictures—after all, it's not necessarily always the equipment, it's whether you have an eye for it or not.

We were getting close to the house number we were looking for when Dad stopped the car as two college-age-looking guys stepped out to cross the street. They had beach towels slung around their necks and bare chests with nice abs, and wore low-riding surf shorts. One of them carried a Frisbee, while another had a volleyball tucked under his arm.

I sat up in the backseat, wondering if that was Adam and Spencer. But no, upon closer inspection, one of them had short, nearly platinum-blond hair, and the other's was brown, shoulder-length—not at all like Spencer and Adam.

Which wasn't a bad thing, because I was looking forward to seeing what guys might be around, too. And I *didn't* mean Dad's college buddies or their sons.

While we were stopped, the guy carrying the volleyball leaned down and peered into the car—I guess he'd caught me staring at him. He smiled at me, then waved with a casual salute.

I smiled and waved back to him. I wanted to take a lot of pictures, so why not start now? I buzzed the window down. "Hold on a second, okay?" I asked. I grabbed my slim, shiny green camera from my bag, and took some quick shots as they played along, grinning and flexing their muscles, showing off a couple of tattoos.

"Emily." My mother peered back at me over the front seat. "What are you doing?"

"Capturing the local flavor," I said as a car behind us honked its horn, and the guys hustled across the street so we could get moving again. "Just trying to blend in with that whole Southern hospitality thing."

"Hmph," my mother said, while my dad laughed.

I turned around and looked out the back window at the guys, wondering if we'd be staying anywhere close by, when Mom shrieked, "Look! There's the house!"

My dad slammed on the brakes, which screeched like the sound of a hundred wailing—and possibly ill—seals. Dad has this awful habit of calling Rent-a-Rustbucket in order to save money. Consequently, we end up driving broken-down automobiles whenever we go on vacation.

Dad backed up and turned into a small parking lot behind the tall, skinny house. I immediately recognized all the *L* bumper stickers and Linden College window-clings on the cars in the lot.

"Look!" Mom pointed at a Linden College banner that was hanging off the third-floor balcony, flapping in the breeze. There was a giant green, leafy linden tree on the dark blue banner background, and in the center, a heart-shaped leaf with a giant *L* in the middle.

Sometimes my dad's Linden school pride got a little ridiculous—for instance, he couldn't possibly get dressed in the morning (at least on weekends and vacations) without donning some piece of Linden College apparel, and he owns about fourteen different ball caps, some faded and tattered and some brand-new—but since I'd actually be going off to school there in the fall, it was kind of a nice feeling to see the banner.

Dad parked the car with a screech of the brakes and we started to climb out. I closed the door, and I swear a piece of the car fell off onto the pavement.

There was a second or two where I was dreading the inevitable hugging and screaming that went along with greeting everyone. Then the back door opened, I saw Adam's dad, and the feeling was over.

"Jay, you could have at least rented a decent car for once in your life," Mr. Thompson said.

"Why change now?" my dad replied as he clapped him on the back.

"Once a cheapskate, always a cheapskate, huh, Emily?" Mr. Thompson gave me a little shoulder hug.

"Don't get me started," I mumbled, looking up at him with a smile.

"Adam just took off on a run down the beach," Mr. Thompson said. "Heather and her mom are off shopping somewhere. I know Adam is psyched to see you."

"Cool." I grinned. Although I hadn't seen Adam for two years, we'd always gotten along pretty well—I figured we still would. Even if we didn't stay in touch very often, we'd known each other so long that it was kind of like being cousins.

Just then the door opened again and Adam's stepmom and his two younger half brothers charged outside. In another minute, it was total chaos, with everyone yelling, hugging, and talking all at once.

Of course, they were talking about how middle-aged and out of shape they'd all gotten, and how many vacation days they got, and whether there was enough beer for the night. What was next? Medicare? Retirement plans?

I had to figure out where the people my actual age had hidden themselves.

As they say on *Grey's Anatomy*: "Stat."

Ten minutes later, after dumping my suitcase in my room, I stood on the giant back deck, overlooking the ocean. There were houses up and down the beach, all looking pretty similar. On one side of us there seemed to be a large, extended family, complete with lots of young kids, grandparents, and about a dozen beach balls and other water toys floating in their pool.

The house on the other side of us had beach towels lined up on the deck railing, flapping in the warm breeze, and a couple of lacrosse sticks, a random collection of Frisbees, and badminton racquets strewn on the deck, along with a cooler and some empty cans of Red Bull and bottles of sports drink. Something about it screamed "young guys" to me, which seemed promising, but maybe I was just being overly hopeful—or naive. Maybe it was actually screaming "old guys who don't recycle."

Down by the ocean, some kids were playing in the sand, building sand castles and moats, while others swam and tried to ride waves on boogie boards.

"I've made a list of top ten Outer Banks destinations. I read eight different guidebooks and compiled my own list," my mom was explaining to Mrs. Thompson when I walked over to them. "We'll need to go food shopping tonight, of course, and make a schedule for who cooks which night."

"Oh, relax, you can do the shopping tomorrow. Things are very casual around here," Mrs. Thompson said to her. "Dinner's already on the grill, put your feet up." She turned to me. "You should go say hi to Adam. He's down there, in the water."

"He is?"

She gestured for me to join her at the edge of the deck. "He's right there. Don't you see him?"

All I could see except for young kids was a man with large shoulders doing the crawl, his arms powerfully slicing through the water. "That?" I coughed. "That person is Adam?"

His stepmom nodded. "Of course."

Wow. Really? I wanted to say. When I focused on him again, as he strode out of the surf, I nearly dropped my camera over the railing and into the sand. "You know what? I think I *will* go say hi." *Hi, and who are you, and what have you done with my formerly semi-wimpy friend?*

I walked down the steps to the beach in disbelief. Last time I'd seen Adam, his voice was squeaking, and he was on the scrawny side—a wrestler at one of the lower weights, like 145. Not anymore. He had muscular arms and shoulders, and he looked about a foot taller than he had two years ago. His curly brown hair was cut short.

You look different, I wanted to say, but that

would be dumb. *You look different and I sound like an idiot, so really, nothing's changed.*

Why was it that whenever I tried to talk to a guy, I started speaking a completely different language? Stupidese?

"Emily?" he asked.

I nodded, noticing that his voice was slightly deeper than I remembered it. It was sort of like he'd gone into a time machine and come out in the future, whereas I felt exactly the same. "Hi."

He leaned back into the surf to wet his hair. "You look different," he said when he stood up.

"Oh, yeah? I do?" *Different how?* I wanted to ask, but that was potentially embarrassing. Different in the way he did? Like . . . sexy? I waited for him to elaborate, but he didn't. "Well, uh, you do, too," I said.

"Right." He smiled, then picked up his towel and dried his hair. As he had the towel over his head, I took the opportunity to check him out again. Man. What a difference a couple years could make. He used to wear wire-rim glasses, but now, apparently, he had contacts, like me.

There was always this really uncomfortable moment when we first tried to talk after not having seen each other for so long.

"So, how are you?" I asked, patting his shoulder, and then we sort of hugged, very awkwardly, the way you hug someone without actually touching them. Sort of like the Hollywood fake-kiss.

"All right, knock it off, you two!" a voice said.

Funny—that didn't *sound* like my mother, but who else would care if I hugged a suddenly semi-hot Adam?

Chapter 2

I turned to look at who was coming toward us, but the sun was in my eyes.

"You guys!" Heather Olsen cried. "It's *me*." She had on a pair of short shorts and a couple of layered tank tops. She ran up to us, and I gave her a big hug, squeezing her tightly.

"Yay, you're here!" I said. "I haven't seen you in forever."

"I know. Isn't it ridiculous, considering how close we live?" she replied.

I gave her another hug, because the last time we'd gotten together wasn't for a vacation—it was for her dad's memorial service nearly a year ago. We hadn't visited much that time, but we'd stayed in close touch throughout the past year with emails. Adam and Spencer hadn't come to the service, only their parents had, because they now lived pretty far away—Adam and his family lived in Oregon, while Spencer's was in Vermont. Heather and I were the ones still sort of near where everyone started out—Madison, Wisconsin, where they'd all moved and rented a house together *after* college and gone to grad school. We still lived in Madison, while Heather and her mom lived in Chicago, which was only about three hours away. Still, we were usually both so busy we didn't see each other often enough.

"What are you—" Adam asked as Heather jumped on his back, like she wanted a piggyback ride. "I wasn't sure you were coming," he said when she dropped off his back and gave him a playful shove.

"Why wouldn't I?" Heather stared at him, hands on her hips. "No. Only kidding. I know why. But the other guys put on the major hard sell, or maybe it was a guilt trip. Anyway, Mom finally agreed. I told her I wanted to see you guys."

"I'm really glad you came," I told her. "It wouldn't be the same, you know. Without you." I felt myself tripping over my tongue. "Right, Adam?"

"Definitely." Adam looked up at a few pelicans flying past. "It wouldn't count as a reunion."

"We have traditions," I said. "You know. You and Spencer make fun of me and Heather until you run out of put-downs, then you resort to practical jokes."

"Me?" Adam turned to me, not looking amused. "No, I don't."

"You do," I said.

"It's a good thing I'm here, because Emily couldn't possibly defend herself on her own, right?" Heather said.

"What? I could too defend myself," I said. I put up my fists, which aren't all that impressive, actually, considering my arms have this certain resemblance to sticks. All the muscle tone I'd had from ballet over the years had started to fizzle, like the deflating air mattress I'd been forced to sleep on the night before at my aunt and uncle's, who live close to the airport.

"Yeah, but not *well*." Heather punched Adam lightly on the arm, which was no longer an arm but a massive bicep. She rubbed her knuckles afterward and looked up at him. "Speaking of self-defense. Work out much?"

"Yeah." He shrugged. "I just finished baseball season."

"I thought they banned steroids in baseball," Heather said.

Adam laughed, looking slightly embarrassed. "Shut up."

"Fine. You know what? I'm starved. When do we eat? I think I saw some brats on the grill."

"What else is new?" I asked, rolling my eyes. "Cheddar or beer style?"

"You can take my dad out of Wisconsin, but you can't take his bratwurst away," Adam said.

Heather started to run back up the stairs to the deck, then she stopped and looked over her shoulder. "Well, come on, guys, I'm not going to eat by myself."

"We're coming," I told her.

"I forgot how she is," Adam commented as we walked over to the stairs together, me loving the feeling of digging my toes into the soft, warm sand. "I mean, maybe it's a good thing she hasn't changed, with everything that's happened."

"How is she?" I asked.

"Like, um, a whirling dervish," Adam said. "Those things that spin around and around."

"Whirling dervish? Wow, have you been taking vocab vitamins along with your steroids?" I asked.

"Shut up." He gave me a playful—but still possibly bruising, with his strength—hip check as we headed up to the deck. "I don't take steroids, okay? I mean, I know guys who've done it and it's disgusting. So let's not talk about that anymore," Adam said in a more serious tone.

"Agreed," I said. "I didn't really think that, you know." Although it had kind of crossed my mind, because I didn't understand how he'd transformed himself. If he'd changed that much . . . what would Spencer look like? "Anyway, let's forget we ever said anything, and just eat."

"Deal." Adam picked up a paper plate and started loading it with food. I followed his lead, taking some of almost everything.

Heather and I sat next to each other on the deck. We both sat cross-legged, in a sort of yoga position. She's tiny—about five feet tall—and used to do gymnastics at the same level I danced—we were both a little obsessed. She'd always been amazingly flexible, and I was, too, so we used to spend these vacations trying to out-bend each other doing splits, back bends, handstands, and anything else we could do to be pretzel-esque. Adam and Spencer had dubbed us the tumbling twins—or maybe it was the tumbling twits. I suddenly couldn't remember.

Maybe there were some things about our last get-together that I'd purposely forgotten, like the look on Spencer's face when I'd awkwardly tried to tell him how I felt—or the look of his back, rather, when he turned away, ignoring me, as if I hadn't said anything. A person can forget a lot in two years. But that? No. And if I hadn't forgotten, I worried he hadn't, either.

Maybe the Flanagans won't come, I thought, looking around at everyone else already gathered. Maybe they decided to stay home. Maybe their car broke down and they'd decided to just can it.

Oh, relax, I told myself as I bit into a cob of buttery corn. *Spencer has moved on, and so have you. You've had tons of other guys in your life since then. Sure. There's that tech guy at the Apple store . . . and the guy at the Starbucks drive-through you flirted with—once—and . . . um . . .*

Adam sat down across from us. "What's wrong with chairs, anyway? You guys against chairs? Wait, I know. You have to stretch. Isn't that what you were always doing?"

"Before I quit gymnastics," Heather said. "Actually, I just didn't see enough chairs."

"When did you quit gymnastics?" Adam asked, sounding genuinely surprised.

"After the accident," she said. "I broke a few ribs, and . . . it hurt to breathe, never mind flip.

Plus I was just ready to make some changes."

Adam nodded. "Yeah. Sorry about that. I mean . . . about everything. Must have been really hard."

There was a long pause. I looked at Adam, then at Heather, then at my plate, wishing I could say something decent that didn't sound completely clichéd.

"You know what?" Heather suddenly looked up at both of us and smiled. "We have to go out tonight."

"We do?" I asked. I hadn't pictured going out and partying as being in the cards, not with the proportion of parents to us. I mean, it was something I'd hoped to achieve, but only in a fantasy, which is the way most of my daring plans occur.

"We do. I mean, do you really want to sit around and listen to the guys all night? First they'll talk about the place where they all lived, and who never washed the dishes, and who did, and who partied the most, and what girl they tried to date but who wasn't interested in any of them—"

We all laughed, but I also couldn't help but wonder if Heather was feeling a little uncomfortable listening to all the guys reminisce, when her dad wasn't around to join in anymore. As much as hearing my dad's stories over and over again annoyed me, at least I still had the chance to listen to them.

I stood up to get a little more food and took a serving of Mrs. Olsen's famous marshmallow Jell-O salad, which she's been making for every get-together since forever, and that I've been eating for about as long.

"When did your mom have time to make this?" I asked Heather, taking a bite.

"This afternoon. We got here earlier today, then went out shopping for new swimsuits," Heather explained. "There are some *amazing* shops around here. Where were you guys when we got here?" she asked Adam.

"Tim and Tyler wanted to go to an amusement park. I think we went on about twelve kiddie pirate rides."

"I can't believe they're already four," I said. "Seems like they were just born, you know?"

"Ha! Maybe to *you*," Adam said.

"I always kind of wanted siblings," I said. "Someone to take the focus off of *me*."

"I hear you," added Heather with a nod.

There was a loud knock on the fence surrounding the pool area. "Anyone here?" a deep voice called through the fence.

"No!" everyone called back at once.

"Thought so. Let's go, Spence," I heard Mr. Flanagan say.

I kind of held my breath. After Adam, I couldn't wait to see what Spencer looked like. Would he have changed that much, too? I was nervous, maybe even dreading it a little bit. What if he'd changed? What if he was even more handsome than he had been at sixteen? Or, potentially worse, even more conceited?

The gate opened—Mrs. Flanagan was towing a large suitcase, while Spencer and his dad carried a kayak over their heads, which they leaned against the fence.

"You kayaked here?" asked Mr. Thompson. "No wonder it took you so long."

"Anything to save gas money," Mrs.

Flanagan answered with a smile.

Spencer was wearing an orange UVM T-shirt and long khaki shorts. He was barefoot. I suddenly remembered how he liked to go barefoot all the time, and wondered how that worked out during the winters. I rarely saw him during the winter. Maybe he had a completely different look.

"You're here!" Heather said, throwing her arms around Spencer.

Spencer stepped back with an awkward smile, escaping Heather's grasp. "Hey."

"Hey?" Heather repeated. "Is that all you're going to say?"

He looked at her and lifted his eyebrows, like he was trying to think of something better to say, but he couldn't. "Sorry about your dad," he said.

"Thanks." Heather hugged him again. "I appreciate that." She let him go and looked up at him. "But I didn't mean that." There was an awkward pause. "Well? Are you going to hug Emily or not?"

Good question, I thought. What was the

etiquette for this kind of situation? It was like Heather could see that things were awkward, but I'd never told her about my dumb confession of love—or was it *like*?—to Spencer two years ago.

He gazed at me for a second, rubbing his eyes, because clearly he'd just woken up after the extremely long car trip. "Emily. That you?" he asked, scratching the side of his face, which looked a little stubbly. He was turning into a grown-up. He had actual stubble.

I laughed. "Of course it's me. Who else would it be? Hi." I punched his arm a little awkwardly, but hit it harder than I meant to, and we sort of hugged, but sort of almost toppled over at the same time.

"Ouch. You're tall," he said.

"Me? No, I'm the same height I used to be," I said, pulling a sticky strand of my hair off of my face.

"You have something in your hair," Spencer said.

"Still?" I pulled at a few more hairs, then found a clump of mini-marshmallows. I could feel myself blush as I attempted to pull them out. Fortunately, I have thickish hair—but unfortunately, it's black, so every speck of marshmallow showed. This wasn't exactly how I'd wanted my reunion with Spencer to go.

"It's the Mello Jell-O," Heather explained to him.

Spencer rubbed his forehead. "The what?"

"My mom's famous mold dessert thingy."

"Your mom serves mold?"

"No, stupid, it's a mold, as in a shape. And it has fruit and marshmallows in it—"

"Oh, yeah. Now I remember. Well, I guess everyone has to be famous for *some*thing."

Heather shoved him. "Are you dissing my mom?"

"No, just gelatin. So what happened? Did you dive into the bowl?" Spencer asked me.

No, I was eating it when you showed up, and I guess I got a little flustered, and my spoon ended up in my hair. "Ha-ha," I said in a deadpan tone. "It's a styling product, okay?"

"Well . . . style away," Spencer said, surveying the deck.

"Same old obnoxious Spencer," Heather muttered under her breath as Spencer left us to get a burger.

It was true that he treated us like we were little kids, even though he was only a year older than us. He usually made a big effort to remind us that he was older. Heather, Adam, and I were just *so* immature. We were like *infants*, compared to him.

The three of us sat down to finish eating dinner, and Spencer joined us. As soon as Heather tossed her paper plate into the trash can, she stood up, looked at the three of us, and said, "What are you guys waiting for? Come on, let's get out of here, go out somewhere fun."

"Go out? But I just got here," Spencer protested. "I don't even know what room I'm in, or where my stuff should go."

"We'll figure it out when we get back. You can unpack later. You've got two weeks to unpack." Heather pulled Spencer to his feet and guided him toward the deck steps.

"Technically, no, because I'll have to unpack in order to change my clothes, like tomorrow," Spencer said. "Anyway, where are we going and what's the rush?"

"I don't know. We'll find a place," said Heather confidently, looping her arm through his.

I interrupted the parents for a second to tell them that the four of us were going for a walk. They barely paused talking long enough to hear what I had to say. Dad mumbled, "That's great, honey," then went back to some story about sophomore year and a football game they lost by one point.

Just before I went to join Spencer, Heather, and Adam, I stopped and took a picture of the three of them as they pushed and shoved each other on the stairs. A lot of things had changed since we first became friends when we were little, but some things hadn't changed at all.

I was starting down the stairs when a Frisbee came sailing over the fence and nearly knocked me in the head. I reached up instinctively to shield my face and the Frisbee hit my hands and fell to the deck.

"Little help?" a guy's voice called over from next door.

"Oh. H-hi," I stammered as he got closer. I wasn't sure, but it looked like the same guy who'd said hi to me earlier in the car—the one with the short, platinum-blond hair.

"Did I see you earlier? You took my picture," he said. "Old car, screechy brakes—that was you, right?"

Thanks, Dad, I thought, *for making such a great impression.* I nodded, feeling flustered.

"You find everything okay?" he asked "Y'all looked a little lost."

Y'all. Was that cute or what? "We were. My dad nearly caused a wreck when he stopped and turned. I think I've got whiplash." *Of course, maybe that was from looking out the back window at you.* "But. Anyway." I laughed. "We made it."

"Cool. Well, ask us if you need to know where to go for stuff. We've already been here a week so we know our way around."

"Great. That'd be, uh, really, uh, helpful," I told him. *Especially if you decided to give me a personal tour of the town.* "Are you, um, here with family, too?" I asked.

"No, friends," he said.

"That sounds fun," I replied. "So, I'm—"

"Emily!" my mom suddenly called over to me. "Don't forget to take your sweater, hon, it might get chilly!"

"I'll be fine!" I called back over my shoulder at my mom. I could have killed her right then. She could be so overprotective that she made me seem a lot younger than I actually was. Half the time, she acted as if I didn't know how to take care of myself.

"Here." He tossed a sweatshirt over the fence. "No need to run for a sweater. Just leave this on the railing here when you get back. Or return it to me tomorrow. Whatever."

"Really? You sure?" *You don't even know me. And I don't know you, though I wouldn't mind.*

"Don't stress. It's yours for the night." He smiled.

"Well, um, thanks. Cool." I was trying to act casual, like this was something that happened to me all the time, when in reality, I'd never worn a guy's clothes before—not any guy I was interested in, anyway. Girls at school were always wearing boyfriends' sweaters and letter jackets and things like that. The closest I'd ever gotten was borrowing Erik Hansen's stocking cap on a biology class field trip when it was ten below. Stocking caps belonging to hockey players weren't exactly sexy. Smelly, yes. "Thanks again. I'm sure I'll be freezing and I'll be, you know, so grateful." I held up the sweat-shirt. "So, see you around . . . ?" I paused, waiting for him to tell me his name.

"No doubt. See you tomorrow!"

Promise? I thought as I watched him fling the Frisbee to his friends on the other side of the deck and they all jogged down the steps to the beach. Maybe this vacation had a lot more in store for me than I'd thought. Maybe instead of just taking pictures of my friends and their boyfriends, I'd be *in* the picture, for a change — with what's his name.

"Come on, Emily! We're waiting!" Heather yelled to me from the town-side of the house, yanking me back to reality.

Chapter 3

"*Y*ou still walk funny," Spencer commented as he followed me into a coffee shop we'd found on the busy main drag, not too far from our rental house.

"Thanks," I said, looking around the place for a table. "Thanks so much."

"So do *you*." Heather jabbed Spencer in the back as we stood at the counter to order.

"It wasn't an insult. I'm just saying she still walks like a ballerina," said Spencer.

"How would you know how a ballerina walks?" asked Heather. "Don't tell me one actually *dated* you."

I didn't give him a chance to answer. "Anyway, it's ballet dancer, not ballerina. Not that I'm particular or anything." I pulled at the light blue sweatshirt I'd wrapped around my waist. *His* light blue sweatshirt. Whoever *he* was. Sigh.

I probably would have worn it no matter what, just because, but the air-conditioning was turned up high—or down low, rather—and I was already freezing, with goose bumps covering my arms. I hate it when my mother turns out to be right, that when she tells me to take another layer, I do turn out to need one. She's spent lots of years being a stage mom, I guess, and she's used to the role even if I've outgrown it.

But if my mother found out I was putting on a sweatshirt that belonged to some guy I didn't even know, she'd have a heart attack—and, at the same time, before she crumpled to the ground, she'd spray me down with extra-strength antibacterial gel.

The cotton sweatshirt material was very soft, like it had been worn and washed a hundred times. I loved how it felt, especially that it was an extra-baggy extra-large. It was like wearing a fleece blanket.

"UNC? Is that where you're going?" Spencer asked, pointing to the initials on the front of the sweatshirt.

"Uh—me? No," I said quickly. I didn't want to tell him that I'd borrowed it from our hot next-door neighbor. For one thing, he wouldn't agree on the "hot" description, and for another, he'd immediately start teasing me about chasing after guys, as if it was something I regularly did. In truth, I only managed to do it on these vacations, with Heather. The rest of my life was usually so over-scheduled that I didn't often have the chance to talk to guys, much less borrow sweatshirts from them. "It's, um, borrowed."

"Borrowed? From who, your dad?" Spencer asked.

"No," I said, not wanting to get into it.

"Oh, my God—it's your boyfriend's, isn't it?" Heather cried. "You finally have a boyfriend and you're holding out on me?" she announced to nearly the entire coffee shop.

Did she have to say "finally"?

I wanted to put up the sweatshirt hood, cover my face with it, draw the strings into a knot, and disappear. "It's not . . . no," I stammered. *At least, not yet.*

Heather peered at me with narrow, suspicious eyes. "Are you sure?"

"Very sure. Let's change the subject," I suggested. I was so embarrassed that I couldn't even look at Adam and Spencer.

"Okay, I'll save you," Spencer volunteered. "So, about that weird walk of yours. Are you still into ballet?"

"I didn't know you cared," Heather teased him.

"I don't. I'm just trying to make conversation that isn't about guys," he said as he stirred a packet of raw sugar into his iced coffee. "So we don't end up discussing all your crushes, like we did on the rest of all our trips."

"Jealous or something? Should we only talk about *you*?" Heather asked, and we all laughed.

"I'm sure we'll be doing that enough," I muttered.

"What's that?" Spencer asked.

"Nothing." I sipped my strawberry smoothie. "Back to ballet. I've really scaled back a lot. I no longer train six hours a day and make my entire schedule around it."

"But you were such a good dancer. Ballerina. Whatever. Weren't you?" asked Adam.

"Thanks, yeah, I was okay. But you know. Things change." I shrugged.

"What happened?" Spencer asked. "I mean, last I knew, you got some big part. That's *all* your parents wrote about in their Christmas letter."

Our parents are all nuts about sending out these long, complicated letters every Christmas to update each other, with embarrassing details about us and our "phases." Heather and I once completely rewrote our parents' letters and sent each other parodies of them. In my version, I'd gone through a brilliant-actor phase and gone on to star on Broadway; in hers, she'd entered a genius phase and become the youngest-ever winner of the Nobel Peace Prize.

"Not this past year—*two* Christmases ago," I corrected him. "I know. And they sent a picture, which I begged them not to do."

Spencer cleared his throat. "It wasn't just one picture. It was a *collage*," he said.

"That wasn't my idea!" I protested, laughing. "Anyway, you know how you can be really into something for a while, and then it's just not your thing anymore."

"Like you and *Sesame Street*," Heather teased Spencer.

"I just realized that it was taking up all my time. You can't do anything else, it's your whole life, which is fine for some people, but it wasn't for me," I said. "I kind of wanted to have a normal life."

"Good luck with *that*," Spencer muttered.

After a while it had been more my mother's dream than my own, to be truthful. I still loved dance and I always would, but there was so much more to me than just ballet. Or at least that's what I thought when I realized I wanted to quit. Other people might see it differently — in fact, *were* seeing it differently. Talk about being typecast.

"So if you're no longer a prima ballerina,"

said Spencer, "what *are* you into?"

"Photography," I said.

"Oh, really? Just that?" asked Spencer.

"Why, what am I supposed to be into?" I retorted.

"Spencer, somehow you can insult people without trying very hard. Have you noticed?" Heather said. "I mean, good luck making friends at college, with that attitude. Speaking of. Where *are* you two going to college?" she asked. "We never heard. Is the reason we don't already know because you didn't get in any-where?"

"Yeah, right," Spencer muttered. "Didn't you get the press release? I'm going to Linden."

I nearly choked on the smoothie sip I'd just taken. *Did he just say "Linden"?* I wondered. *Maybe he said Clinton. Or London.*

"Wait a second," I said. "I thought you were at the University of Vermont."

"You're transferring?" asked Heather, not sounding nearly as stunned as I did. "Cool! You'll be a sophomore there, so you can be our cool, older friend. Well, older anyway."

"But I thought you were at UVM," I said again. "I mean, you have the shirt. And everything."

"And you have a UNC sweatshirt and that doesn't mean anything, does it?"

"No, but—"

"Anyway, I won't be a sophomore, because I changed my mind and took the last year off to volunteer. I'll be a freshman like you guys, well, except I have some AP credits, and I'll still be older than you, and therefore more mature, and you'll be lucky if I talk to you at Linden," Spencer said, then he smiled. "Kidding."

"We're going to be so popular, you'll be lucky if we talk to *you*," Heather replied.

I tried not to think of how weird that would be, at a small school with Spencer, the guy I'd made my one and only pass at. Would I have to bribe him to keep it to himself?

Then again, maybe he didn't even really remember. It had been the last night of our trip to the Dells when I blurted out how we should stay in touch and how we were such a good match. I'd still had that electrified feeling—

maybe *fried* was a better word for it—when I first saw him today, but who knew what he was up to these days? Maybe he had a serious girl-friend back home. I'd have to find out.

Anyway, I'd had serious changes in my life, too, since then. Serious relationships. Okay, mostly just in my mind, but still.

Linden only had about 1,100 students, but it wasn't that small a campus. It wasn't as if he'd be in all my classes. He'd probably stay away from me—far away.

"So what did you do all last year, then? As a volunteer?" I asked.

"I worked in New Orleans on hurricane relief projects—building houses, rebuilding schools—"

"Then how come your parents didn't mention *that* in their holiday letter?" Heather teased.

"My parents don't send a holiday letter," he said.

"Oh. So *they're* the normal ones," I observed. Spencer already seemed conceited enough, so I didn't tell him how cool I thought that was, that he took time off to help other people. That was the kind of thing I'd totally wanted to do myself, but I didn't have the guts to just put my life on hold. He did. "So what exactly made you volunteer?" I asked.

"Um, I don't know." He fiddled with the napkin under his coffee cup. He looked a little flustered by the question. "Just, you know. Seemed like I could use a break from school and my community center was sending people to help, so . . ."

Heather started to smile. "So let me get this straight. You'll be a freshman, like us. You, who've tortured us and taunted us every year about being so much *older* than us—"

"Which I still am. And I might be a freshman, but I couldn't be like you guys even if I tried."

"Oh, of course not. Never." I rolled my eyes. "Heather, how in the world are we ever going to fit our baby cribs and playpens into our dorm rooms?"

She smiled. "So what about you, Adam?"

Heather asked. "Oh, wow. Don't tell me we're all going to Linden. Is it something they put in our drinking water?"

"Um. Speaking of water. Does anyone else besides me need some?" Adam started to get up and head to the counter.

"Dodging the question, huh?" Heather prodded.

"I was trying to," he said with an awkward laugh as he sat back down. "I don't know where I'm going to end up in the fall. Actually I got into Oregon State, but I'm, um, wait-listed at Linden. But I'm sure I'll get in. Totally. Just mailed in my application late, that's all. They're going to give me a hard time about it and make me wait. I'm a legacy—we all are. They always let in legacies." He coughed. "Right?"

My cell started ringing. It was my dad's ring tone—I have it set to the Linden school song. When everyone heard that, they started laughing and accusing me of being obsessed already.

"Where are you?" Dad asked.

"We're having coffee," I said.

"Coffee? You don't drink coffee at night," he said.

Somehow that made him worry that I wasn't telling the truth. "What, do you think I'm making that up? Okay, so the deep dark truth is that I'm having a smoothie. At a coffee *shop*," I said. "And afterward we're going to walk around and check out the area."

"Check out what?" Dad asked.

I swear he's not that old and hard of hearing. I just have a crummy phone. Again, my parents tend to opt for the bargains in life — with the exception of what they'd spent over the years on ballet, for me. The phone had been "refurbished," but apparently its first owner was an octopus, or someone who spent a lot of time in the sea. It had a constant bubbling sound in the background.

Heather grabbed the phone from me and said, "We haven't seen each other in forever, Mr. Matthias. We have a lot to talk about, okay?"

I could hear my dad laughing over the phone as they spoke for a minute, then Heather handed it back to me. "We'll be back soon," I promised.

"Parents still a little overprotective, huh?" asked Adam as I slipped my phone back into my pocket.

"A smidge," I said. Over the past year, my parents had been gradually adjusting to the fact that my social life wasn't entirely about ballet anymore. They were having a hard time with the fact they couldn't always reach me at the studio, where I'd be hanging out with three other dancers. Even if there were guys around—like an occasional partner from time to time—usually they weren't my type, or rather, I wasn't theirs.

"Don't worry, we can always sneak out later." Heather picked up her coffee cup and slid her handbag over her shoulder.

"We can?" I asked.

"Sure. Didn't you see how many *doors* that house had? There's no way they can keep track of us every second." She smiled, then put her arm around my shoulder and we sort of danced out of the coffee shop.

We headed back to the house, and Heather and I caught up some more while Adam and Spencer walked ahead of us, having an in-depth discussion about baseball. I think. I never watch baseball, so I had no idea what they were talking about, actually.

"Okay, so here's the way I see it." Heather smoothed her long blond hair back into a bar-rette. We'd always been complete opposites: She was blond, I was brunette; she was loud, and I was quiet; she was bold and I was, well, faint. Un-bold.

"We're here for our last real vacation before we head to college, which will be very serious and boring and not fun," Heather continued.

"It will? What about the parties?" I asked. "The football games, the frats—you know, all the things our dads—" I caught myself, feeling horribly insensitive. "The stuff the guys go on and on about, reliving their glory days."

"Just work with me for a second. What I'm trying to say is that we have fourteen days here, so let's find some amazing guys to have summer flings with. Are you in?"

"Uh . . . is that the plan?" I asked. She made it sound so easy.

"Pretty much. I'll help you find a guy, and you'll help me find one, which shouldn't be that hard because it seems like there are tons of them around here on vacation just like us. . . ."

"True," I agreed, thinking of our hot next-door neighbor, whatever his name was.

"And we'll just have one of those painstakingly sad brief summer love affairs—"

I laughed. "You've been watching too many movies," I said. "That doesn't happen in real life."

"What do you know about real life, anyway? You've been stuck in a dance studio the past five years," Heather teased.

"Hm. You might have something there," I agreed.

"You have perfect posture and positions, and like, no dates," Heather said. "Am I right?"

"Well, you don't have to make me sound that pathetic," I replied with a laugh.

She laughed, too. "Hey, I'm only saying that because I know that's how *I* was with

46

gymnastics. I spent every summer at gymnastics camp, every afternoon training. . . . I loved it, but it puts some serious limits on your social life."

"True." I remembered wishing I didn't have so many commitments, that I had time to just hang out at the mall and boy-shop with my friends.

"Anyway. This will be something short, just a fling. It's not something that you're going to continue, like a relationship or whatever. I mean, I guess if it worked out, and you didn't live completely on other sides of the country — but be realistic. We're going off to college and we're not going to be tied down to some guy who isn't even *there*."

I stopped walking and looked at her. "Wow. You *have* thought about this a lot. Did you map out the whole thing, like what we say and when we say it?" *Because I can use that kind of help,* I thought. A sheet of instructions. No, a booklet. And a website with updates.

"Shut up, it was a long plane ride this morning. I had time," she said. "So. We'll get started first thing tomorrow. What we need to do is meet some guys and—"

"I already met someone," I admitted.

"Are you kidding?" She pushed me. "When?"

"Right when we were leaving tonight! I almost got my head cut off by a Frisbee, but it was worth it, because I met the guy next door. Really nice. He loaned me this sweatshirt."

"So that's where you got it," she said, nodding. "*Really*. Well, this sounds promising! So what was his name?"

"Name? Well, um . . ."

"You didn't get his *name*?" Heather demanded.

"I didn't tell him my name, either, so—"

"And that makes it *right*?"

"He's staying next door to us. We'll see him again."

"Still. You ask a guy's name. It lets them know you're interested. I mean, are you with me, or not?"

"Fine. I'll get his name first thing tomorrow," I promised.

I wasn't planning to tell Heather how clueless I was about dating, but I didn't think I'd need to. She could tell.

To, tell the truth, I was starting to think that I'd head to college without ever having had a real boyfriend—and a date at the seventh-grade dance didn't count.

That sounded so, so wrong. And so very, very likely.

But it wasn't as if I'd *tried* to be single. Forever. It just worked out that way. And it wasn't only the Spencer incident, where I'd failed miserably.

When I was a junior, there was this one British guy I totally loved named Gavin. He moved. To Arizona. I mean, what were his parents thinking, moving to Arizona, when he's British? For some reason he belonged more in Wisconsin. Because of me, because I was there. Not that I ever managed to talk to him for more than ten minutes, and not that I ever had the nerve to ask him out. But still, I loved him. Deeply.

Then, on a more serious note, there was my

friend Terence, who lived down the block and who I used to spend all my time with. At one point senior year I realized that I loved him also. Like, in the way that you shouldn't love a guy who's essentially your best friend. I kept trying to tell him how I felt, but I couldn't, and then he went out with my friend Shauna. Which wasn't fair at all, because I knew him a lot longer than she did, and all of a sudden we weren't allowed to hang out as much as we used to.

Anyway, the whole Terence and Shauna situation was over now—they'd broken up after only two months together—but I still have a heart scar from that.

Maybe a fling *was* the answer. A fling in which nobody got deeply involved and, therefore, nobody got hurt. And one in which I never had to tell a guy how I felt or how long I'd felt that way or hear him say sorry, but he didn't have the same feelings for me.

I hated the word "feelings," come to think of it.

"Define 'fling,'" I said to Heather as we walked up the steps onto the deck at the back of the house. "Because 'fling' is 'feeling' without the two *e*'s."

"Actually any good fling should have a couple *e*'s in it. Like, 'ee, this is fun, ee, he's kidding me—'"

"*Kidding* me? That doesn't sound fun," I commented, laughing.

"*Kissing* me, I meant to say. Give me a break, I have jet lag," Heather said. "You know, it's a romantic evening. You hold hands. You gaze at each other." She shrugged. "You act and feel goofy. You kiss. Dance, maybe."

"That's it?" I asked, climbing into a chair beside the pool.

"The rest is optional." She sat down beside me in a chaise lounge chair. "Fun, but optional."

We both laughed.

"*Have* you . . . ? I mean, would you . . . ?" I whispered.

"No. I've had the chance, but you know, the person—the timing—it wasn't right. And I definitely don't think it's something you should do on, like, vacation. With some guy you don't really know all that well."

"Agreed," I said.

"But you could make out."

I leaned back and looked up at the sky. "Right."

"And if you got carried away . . ."

"No." I shook my head. "Still not. Too risky." The whole thing sounded too risky, if you asked me. If I didn't do well with guys I already knew, how would I handle things any better with strangers?

But I'd try to follow Heather's lead, the way I did every time we were on vacation together. When we were about eight, she dared me to eat ten red-hot fireball candies in a row, so I did. That same trip, she dared me to jump off a tire swing into a lake, and I did that, too.

I ended up with a burning-hot mouth and a red stomach from belly-flopping. That was when I decided that maybe Heather wasn't the best role model for me.

But maybe there were events worth following her in. And if Heather could find a guy to have an innocent—or fairly innocent—summer fling with, why couldn't I?

Besides, I'd already met someone. For once, I was a step ahead of *her*.

"What are you guys so busy talking about?" Mrs. Olsen had walked out onto the deck, followed by my mom.

"You could have told us the bad news, Mom," Heather said.

Mrs. Olsen looked a bit panicked for a second. "What bad news?"

"That Spencer's following us to Linden."

My mother laughed. "What? I, for one, think it's wonderful news," she said. "Don't you think so, Emily?"

I thought that it was strange. Weird. Potentially nice, because it never hurts to know lots of people. And potentially very embarrassing, because sometimes it's the wrong kind of people, the ones you'll never, ever turn to because they'd mock you for it.

"Sure, Mom. It's wonderful," I murmured, glancing over at Spencer. Absolutely, positively, wonderfully *bizarre*.

Heather suddenly jumped up and grabbed hold of my hands. "Come on, Em, let's go."

"What?"

"We need to talk some more—in private," she said under her breath as she pulled me by the wrist. "We need a plan of attack, don't you think? We're just going down to the beach, stick our toes in the water!" she announced over her shoulder to everyone.

"If you're not back in fifteen minutes, I'm sending someone after you!" my mother called.

"Fine. Just send someone cute from next door," Heather added and we laughed as we ran down the steps toward the ocean.

Chapter 4

"*E*mily! Emily!"

I turned my head and slid my sunglasses down my nose to see who was calling my name. I was lying in a bikini on the beach with an open book across my bare stomach—I guess I'd fallen asleep while I was reading.

When I could focus, I saw that it was the guy from next door. I couldn't believe it. The same guy who'd loaned me his UNC sweatshirt, and before that, nearly decapitated me with a Frisbee. He was jogging down the beach toward me, wearing shorts, no shirt, with a striped beach towel slung around his neck, calling my name. "Em-i-ly! Em-i-ly!"

I quickly sat up, then jumped up from my

own striped beach towel and hurried toward him. I ran faster and faster, but my feet kept slipping in the sand. I looked down and realized I had my ballet slippers on, and then I realized I was late for a performance and not only that, I was wearing a bikini instead of my tutu. My trig teacher appeared out of nowhere, asking for my homework. I just ran past her and leaped into his arms.

"Hey." He wrapped his arms around my waist and I put my arms around his strong shoulders and he pulled me closer. He lifted me in the air and tried to twirl me around, but unfortunately, something kept getting in the way. Something was wrapped all around my legs and I suddenly couldn't move. Seaweed—monster-size seaweed—was about to strangle me.

I sat bolt upright.

I wasn't on the beach.

I was in bed.

Alone. Very, very alone. And I was tangled up in my bedsheets. There was a magazine on my stomach, which I'd been reading the night before.

Well, at least I hadn't failed trig or ended up onstage in a bikini.

It took me a second to figure out where I was. I don't know if it's because I'm a photographer or what, but it seems like I have the most vivid, visual—and unusual—dreams. Sometimes it can really freak me out because I can't tell what's real and what isn't.

Unfortunately, the dream about next-door guy wasn't real. The scene of me waking up wrapped like a mummy in my sheets—that was.

Shoot. No pun intended. I'd planned to get up early and photograph the sunrise. I glanced at the alarm clock and saw that I was about four hours late for that. What had happened? Then again, if I'd been having dreams like that, no wonder I stayed asleep.

I quickly got dressed, throwing on a pair of white shorts and a pink polka-dot bikini top. The temp outside seemed pretty hot when I opened a window to quickly check it. Besides, I wanted to meet guys, right? When in Rome, and when on the Outer Banks, and all that.

I left my room and walked out into the

fourth-floor hall. The house was four stories, with two large kitchens on the first and third floors. Each family had at least one room, or suite, with an attached bathroom—and some had two, like ours. It was sort of like being inside a hotel that was inside of a house. I was so happy that I didn't have to share a room with my parents—I had a small bedroom with a miniature bathroom, sort of like a little attic afterthought. The only other person on the fourth floor, with a similar room, was Adam. His door was closed, and I wondered if he—and everyone else in the house—was already up, outside, and on my mom's latest adventure. *Why hadn't she woken me up?* I wondered. That wasn't like her. Normally she'd pound on my door until I was up. Besides, she had Big Plans for this trip. Things we absolutely had to see.

I went to the third-floor kitchen, located the coffeemaker, and poured myself a mugful. Then I wandered over to the window to look out at the ocean (my bedroom faced the other way, toward the parking lot) and saw Adam's little brothers playing in the pool below, with the Thompsons and my mom and dad nearby. I wondered if the guy next door was up yet. Probably—everyone else seemed to be.

"Sleep much?" A voice behind me nearly made me jump through the window.

I struggled to keep from spilling my coffee. I turned to find Spencer, who I hadn't noticed sitting on the sofa in the attached living room. "You scared me!"

He looked up from the book he was reading. "You scared *me*," he replied. "Have you seen your hair?"

"Shut up." I glanced at my reflection in the oven door and ruffled my hair a little to make it fall more neatly. I guess I hadn't really paid much attention to it. "Heather and I stayed up late last night talking," I explained.

"Really," he said. "She's already out playing volleyball."

"With who?" I asked.

"Some guys. I think they live next door," Spencer said. "Typical Neanderthals."

"Do we have something against

Neanderthals?" I asked. "Do we have a complex or something?"

"Complex. Not usually a word I associate
with Neanderthals," Spencer mused.

I opened the sliding glass door and walked
out onto the upper deck for some fresh air—
and a better view. Down on the beach, Adam,
Heather, and a couple of guys were playing
against my platinum-blond friend and some
other people.

So it's true, I thought. *The early bird catches the
hot boy.* Or something like that. What was I
thinking, sleeping in, when this was waiting for
me on the beach?

I closed the door and ran upstairs to get
my camera, then hurried back down, and out
onto the lower-level deck. Before they noticed
me, I managed to get a few quick shots of
everyone. When Heather saw me, she stopped
to wave, and the volleyball nearly nailed her in
the face. My photo captured her sprawling to
the ground, to get out of the way, but grabbing
one of the guy's arms as she fell. I didn't know

whether it was intentional or not, but her move sure worked, and they laughed and fell onto the sand together.

"Hey! How's it going?" my sweatshirt-lending friend called over to me.

"Hi!" I waved back to him. "Great shot!" I said, but the wind caught my hair and whipped it into my mouth, so it came out as more like "GWMFPT!"

"Game's almost over!" he called back.

I wanted to take a picture of him. What could I tell him to get him to pose? *I'm taking pictures to make a calendar and I want you to be Mr. July?*

I kept the lens trained on him, catching a few good action shots before the game was over and they stopped for a break. He jogged over to me, with Heather right beside him.

"Emily, this is Blake," said Heather.

Was it me, or was it completely wrong that she was introducing me to the guy that *I'd* met?

Not that she wouldn't have met him on her own, without me. But still. Just because

I hadn't been clever or suave enough to find out his name—and wake up before ten in the morning—that didn't mean they were supposed to be hanging around without me.

Blake introduced me to his friends, all of whom seemed to have Southern accents as well, from the hardly noticeable lilt to a heavy drawl.

"Oh, hold on a second—I have your sweatshirt." I raced up to the deck to retrieve it. Unfortunately, the sweatshirt had fallen off onto the ground below, plus it had rained overnight, so it was sopping-wet, dirty, and covered with sand.

I wasn't sure he'd want it back now, but I walked over to him, holding it out. "Here's your sweatshirt." I looked around, wondering where Heather had gone.

He frowned at me, then gradually his mouth turned upward into a smile. "Remind me never to give you my clothes again."

I smiled, feeling my face turn warm, then hot, then scorching. "You know what? Why don't I see if there's a washer and dryer here—

I can clean it and get it dry and then bring it back to you," I offered.

Blake shook his head. "Don't worry about it. I'll just leave it here in the sun to dry. No problem."

"You sure?" I asked.

"I'm sure." He nodded with a nice smile. "Hey, before I forget—what are y'all doing tomorrow night?"

"Um, I—I don't know yet," I stammered. "Why?"

"We're having a party. You should come!"

"Really?" I asked. "I mean, that sounds great. Cool." There was a slight pause. "Uh, thanks. We'll look forward to it."

"Don't expect too much. Just a casual, you know, thing. What are you up to this morning?" he asked.

"I'm not sure. My mom—she tends to plan everything to the hilt, so I'm sure there's something," I said.

We stood side by side, toes in the wet sand, the incoming waves washing over our feet. Where in the world was Heather? Did she expect me to do this all by myself?

"So, where are you guys from?" asked Blake.

"All over, actually," I said. "I'm from Wisconsin—"

"No kidding? I went there once."

"Once?" I smiled. "Only once?"

"It was winter. I didn't want to go back," Blake said, and we both laughed. "I think it was a *high* of ten. I'm not cut out for that. I grew up in Savannah," he said in his devastatingly cute Southern accent. "Y'all should move. Like, before winter."

Another "y'all." I could kiss him just on the basis of how cute that sounded. Not that it was anything I'd ever done before, just randomly kiss someone, but hey—what was I waiting for?

"I've tried to convince them, believe me," I told Blake. "I once had an entire lobbying plan to get us all to move to California. Everyone loved the idea, except, well, my mom and dad. My cat loved the idea."

He smiled, picking up a shell and skipping it across the incoming wave. "So how do you survive and have fun?"

"You learn to wear layers. Sometimes you're wearing so many layers you can't move," I explained. "So, um. Have you been here before? To this place?"

"Once before, when I was a little kid. Maybe six. And then my buddy Trevor—he's the one with the long brown hair. His family has a house here—that house, I mean. We're friends from UNC."

"Cool," I commented, sounding uncool.

"So, are you going to school anywhere warm, at least? Like, I don't know. Alaska?" Blake teased me.

"Not quite. Northern Michigan," I said.

"Ouch. Y'all *are* crazy." He laughed. "Well, you can always transfer. You could be a Tarheel."

"A what?"

"That's what they call us at UNC. Tarheels."

I peered down at his foot and saw that his ankle had a light black, slightly faded tattoo around it. I couldn't see what shape it was, exactly. "I don't see any tar," I said. "Maybe you're more of a sand heel?"

"Yo, Blake! Let's move! Tee time in ten!"

"We're going golfing. Hey, see y'all for beach volleyball later, all right?"

"Sure—sure thing," I said, not that I played beach volleyball, or any kind of volleyball. But I'd try. "Sounds great!"

"Cool. Later, Em!" he called with a little wave over his shoulder.

Great. Sounds . . . great. Also? Looks *great*, I thought as I watched him jog up the steps to his house's deck, and that was the last I could see of him.

"Emily. Emily!" My mother suddenly appeared, waving a brochure in front of my face. "Earth to Emily! We're going on a lighthouse tour this morning. Well, what's left of the morning. Then we'll go out for lunch, so why don't you go get dressed?" she asked.

I glanced down at my clothes. "I am dressed."

She cleared her throat. "*More* dressed."

"Mom, it's the beach, it's vacation," I argued. "Everyone here dresses really casually."

"Yes, but where we're going they might have the AC on. You'd freeze." She flashed a tight-lipped smile at me, and then pointed to the house. "Go change, or at least find another layer."

As much as I loved my mom, I was really looking forward to *not* being told what to do all the time, come fall. I might be homesick, living away from home for the first time ever, but I could use a little freedom in my life. Plus, my mom had this image of me as a fourteen-year-old in her head that she could not seem to get out. I was perpetually fourteen, being driven to lessons or going to the city to watch performances or spending vacations at ballet camp, all arranged by her. Not that I had a problem with it at the time—but in retrospect? I'd have to say my life was a little one-sided back then. I'd missed junior prom to appear in a dance recital. Need I say more?

I was on the way to reconfigure my outfit when I saw Spencer staring out at the ocean from the upstairs deck, where he was standing, book in hand. "You going with us?" I called up to him.

"Going with you where?" he replied.

"Lighthouses," I said. "Or at least one. Then lunch, I guess."

"Do I have a choice?" Spencer asked.

"Not according to her." I pointed to my mother. "*Everyone's* going."

"Then I'd hate to be left behind," he said. "But, you know, if you've seen one lighthouse, you've seen 'em all. And I hate feeling like such a tourist."

"So . . . don't come, then," I suggested.

"Why wouldn't I come? I mean, just because I might hate every second, that's no reason not to come along."

I looked at him, wondering when he'd turned into such an antisocial being. "You're weird. You realize that, don't you?"

"Oh, sure. I'm very, very strange," he said.

"Well, as long as you can admit it." I hurried into the house. On the stairs, I ran into Heather, who had already changed out of her sand-covered clothes and was on her way down. "Did I see you talking to Blake out there?" she asked.

"Yeah. What happened to you?"

"I was too sticky—I had to change. So, how'd it go?"

"You know what? He's really nice," I said.

"Awesome. Did you get his number?"

"No," I admitted. "Anyway, why do we need his number? He's next door!"

"Emily. Are you completely clueless?" she asked. "You get a guy's phone number. It tells him you're interested."

"Oh. Well, I got his name," I said in self-defense, somewhat feebly, knowing she was right about the clueless aspect.

"No, *I* got his name," Heather corrected me with a playful swat on my arm.

"Right." I laughed. "Well, I did talk to him, and he invited me—us—to a party they're having tomorrow night."

"You're kidding!" Heather said.

"Like, oh, my God!" Spencer squealed, coming up the stairs behind me.

Heather turned and gave him a disparaging look. "Who invited you? This is a private conversation."

"Then don't have it on the stairs. Because other people have to use them," Spencer said. "I'm only getting ready because she told me to." He pointed at me. "But you're going to do it again, aren't you?"

"Do what?" I asked.

"Spend the trip being boy crazy," Spencer said. "Just like last time."

"No, not like last time," Heather said.

I coughed. "Definitely not."

"Unlike you, *we've* actually gotten more mature," Heather said. "So it's not the same thing as being what you call 'boy crazy,' because that was us when we were eleven."

"Fifteen," Spencer coughed.

"Plus, we go out more often. Unlike you, I'm betting," Heather said.

"We do?" I said. "Right. We do. All the time. Constantly going out."

Spencer laughed in my face. "Yeah. Right."

How was it he could always manage to see right through me?

And how was it that I didn't punch him?

Chapter 5

"Everybody say 'squeeze!'"

"Squeeze!" Heather and Adam yelled, while Spencer stood a little sullenly off to one side. I didn't mind. I was actually getting good shots of him being less posed. This way, I'd get his true, miffed, unpleasant expression.

"Whatever happened to saying cheese?" he complained.

"We're from Wisconsin," I reminded him. "People call us cheeseheads. It's a bad stereotype."

"Too cheesy," Heather said.

We were standing on the observation deck of Currituck Lighthouse, and so far I'd taken pictures of everything: the tall grasses below, the ocean sound between the strips of land, the lighthouse and its 214 spiral steps to the top, which had made us all break a sweat but had given me very cool photos.

Before the lighthouse tour, we'd gone on a short hike, looking for the wild mustangs that supposedly roamed the area. We only ended up seeing one horse, and it was so hot and buggy that we'd made a dash for the van after not too long. My dad wouldn't stop singing this old U2 song, "Who's Gonna Ride Your Wild Horses?", only changing the lyrics to "Who's gonna find those wild horses?"

My dad has to sing a lot. In public. It doesn't make sense, given the fact he's an accountant, and they're supposed to be stable, boring types. It's because he was in a band in college—I've seen the videos and he wasn't half bad (back then, anyway).

Still, despite my dad's occasional bursting into song, I'd gotten a sense of how beautiful the area was, and how amazing it must have been in the past, before people like us were tromping all over the place, scaring off the wild horses.

"*Take* it already," Spencer said to me. "How many group photos do we need?"

"I'm getting it. I want the shot to be perfect," I said. "We need the lighthouse in the background and—"

Spencer let out a loud and overly obvious sigh. "It's like I said. Seen one lighthouse, you've seen them all," he said.

"Your enthusiasm is so refreshing," Heather commented, shoving him so hard that he moved out of my view just as I pressed the button.

"Perfect," I said. I turned off my camera and put it into my bag. "So, what's next?"

"We have to meet at the van at one," Adam said. "According to your mom. Who told me that about six times."

"Why do I feel like we're on a school field trip?" Heather asked.

"I know," said Spencer. "We have to take off on our own tomorrow. It's not like we don't have enough vehicles—and do we really have to go everywhere together?"

"My mom would never let me leave the group," I began to explain.

"Mine either," Heather added.

Spencer stepped back, putting his hand on his chest. "Not even with a reliable older person like me?"

I shook my head.

He looked a little shocked. "What, I'm not good enough?"

"Please. You're only ten months older than us," I said.

"If that," added Heather.

"I think I know when my birthday is," Spencer said with a laugh.

"Look, who cares? We can always just ask if we can go somewhere together without parental supervision," Adam said. "We'll phrase it in a way that they'll have to say yes. We'll tell them we're going somewhere safe."

"And won't we be?" I asked, wondering what exactly he had in mind.

"Sure, of course. I just meant . . . they might not like the concept of us all going scuba diving or something like that."

"Great idea—I've always wanted to try

that," said Spencer.

"Me too," added Heather. "Love those fins. Dead sexy."

"Oh, yeah, we'll go scuba diving. We'll *totally* do that," I said.

"Why not? It's a great idea," Spencer said.

"It's not a great idea. Trust me. You'll have a mysterious accident somewhere off the pier," I said. "You'll end up on *Dateline NBC*."

"No, you will," Spencer said. "As a . . . a *fun* predator. Someone who tries to find and then kill all the fun." He stared at me, and I felt very uncomfortable all of a sudden.

"Me? I'm no fun-killer," I said. "You're the one who hates lighthouses and refuses to get in the picture."

"I'm just thinking ahead. I can see you Photoshopping me into something really embarrassing."

I took out my camera and turned it back on. "I hadn't thought of that yet, but thanks for the suggestion." I started to focus on Spencer again, noticing the small scar near his left ear where he'd gotten cut when we had a winter reunion once and he sliced his face with an ice skate in a bad fall. This will probably sound weird, but I loved that scar. I could look at it forever. It reminded me of being kids together and how easy it was to just play all day long, without ever having to talk or delve into anything deeper than whether we wanted fries or onion rings with our lunch. (Me: fries; Spencer: onion rings; Heather: celery sticks; Adam: ketchup.) And in another way, something about it was sort of sexy, too.

"Quit it!" Spencer said, pushing my arm to try to get the camera, which I was still pointing at him, lost in memory—or something like it. "What about you, why don't you get in the picture?" We were suddenly wrestling for my little camera, and I was so worried it would fall to the ground and break that I wrapped my arms around his waist and tried to trap him by the edge of the lighthouse wall.

"Okay, you guys, lighten up. We don't need someone falling off the edge." Adam grabbed my arm and separated us.

"What is with you guys? Let's quit arguing and focus, here. Suppose we do get a car." Heather took a pack of gum out of her pocket and popped a square piece into her mouth. "Which is a great idea, but like it or not, we're going to be traveling as a pack. Where should we go?"

"I've studied the guidebook, and there are lots of possibilities," said Spencer.

I sighed. "I'm sure my mother's already planned group outings to all of them."

"That doesn't mean we can't go twice," Spencer argued. "We'd see things differently. You guys are too pessimistic."

"No, more like realistic." Heather offered the gum to the rest of us.

"I'm thinking of another *r* word, actually," Spencer said as he took a piece.

I looked over at Heather. "He must mean ravishing."

"Or else really, really, r—"

"Revolting?" suggested Adam.

"Rigid." Spencer stood ramrod straight, arms at his side.

"You guys fight like two old married couples," my dad commented as he passed by us.

The four of us looked at each other, and Spencer made an exaggerated shiver.

Oh, yeah, like it was such a horrible thought. He could be so arrogant. How could I even have cared about him or his stupid scar, once upon a time?

"Excuse us," said Heather. "We have to get back to our actual *life*." She dragged me toward the spiral staircase. "Everyone knows that if you want to find out where to go in a place, you ask the locals. So, let's find some."

I followed her down the winding stairs, noticing that there were some okay-looking guys on their way up, and wondering if we should turn around and follow *them*.

We stopped outside the lighthouse door and surveyed the parking lot.

All I saw was a steady stream of tourists, mostly of the middle-aged variety. Cars with Ohio, Illinois, and New York license plates cluttered the parking lot, and several people who passed us looked as if they hadn't seen the sun in months—or a lighthouse, judging from their excitement.

"Do they look local?" I asked, pointing to a couple of guys on bicycles coasting into the parking lot. We watched as they rode up to an ice-cream vendor parked in the lot.

"Who cares *where* they live?" said Heather, and she dragged me over to where they stood in line, casually slipping into place behind them. Before I could think of a way to meet them, of anything slightly witty or interesting to say, Heather tapped the taller one on the shoulder. He turned around, a confused look on his face.

"Yeah?"

"Hey." Heather smiled up at him—he was at least a foot and a half taller than her. "I was just wondering, um, where are you guys staying? Because we totally want to rent bikes, too, but we don't know where."

"They're not rented," he said. "They're ours. We live here."

"Oh, you live here? Really? How cool," Heather said.

"Really cool," I added before I could stop myself from saying something so ridiculously redundant. They both looked at me as if I were a bit short in the IQ department.

"We could give you the names of a couple of rental places," his friend suggested.

"That would be great. Thanks. So, where do people go here in Corolla?" Heather asked. "I mean, for fun."

"It's pronounced Cur-all-a. Not Corolla, like the car," the taller one said. "Not that anyone *cares*," he muttered to his friend.

Somehow I didn't think we would end up going anywhere with these guys. They already thought we were idiots.

"We care," Heather told him. "We're going to college in this town in Michigan that nobody can pronounce—Pishnachaumegon."

"Bless you," the taller guy teased, and we all laughed.

"See? We understand," Heather said. "So can you tell us—where should we go? I mean, where do people here go at night?" Heather pressed. "Or, I guess we're staying in Kill Devil Hills, a little south. So what's down there?"

They started rattling off names of places, clubs, and it struck me they were probably old enough to *go* to bars, whereas we weren't even close.

Heather must have had the same thought, because she stopped jotting down names on her arm, and said, "You know, I almost forgot. There's this party tomorrow night. Not at our house, but next door."

My eyes widened. What was she doing?

"Seriously?" asked the taller one.

She nodded. "We're staying on the beach— come find us, we'll hit the party." She quickly jotted down the address on the edge of a lighthouse brochure, then added her cell phone number and handed it to him. "My name's Heather, and this is Emily."

"Hey. I'm Dean," he said. "This is Chase."

"Nice to meet you," I said.

"Call us if you're in the neighborhood, okay?" Heather said, smiling up at Dean.

"Cool." He nodded, and sounded genuine when he said, "We will."

"See you later!" Chase held up his cone in a kind of toast motion to us, then they got back onto their bikes and rode off. They managed to hold their ice-cream treats in one hand and steer with the other, something I'm sure I could never accomplish, and definitely not with people watching me.

Heather and I laughed as she grabbed our ice creams and we walked over to where the guys were waiting for us, outside the van.

Spencer was leaning against the van, foot propped behind him. "Don't tell me you just tried to pick up a couple of guys at the ice-cream truck. That's so middle school of you."

"We didn't," Heather said.

"Good." Spencer nodded.

"We didn't *try*, I mean." Heather smiled, then we both burst out laughing again. "We succeeded," she said.

"Yeah, right," Adam scoffed. "That's why they rode away at top speed."

"You don't know anything," I said. "They're

coming to the party tomorrow."

"What party?"

"The one next door at Blake's. I invited them," Heather announced.

"I hate to have to point this out, but . . . that's not your party," Spencer said. "How could you invite them?"

"Oh, come on. You know how these beach things are. Totally casual, laid back. Haven't you ever watched a surfer movie? So," Heather said, turning to me. "Which one do you want?"

"Which one? Um, how about the sherbet—"

"Not that, silly. The guys." Heather handed me the cup of rainbow sherbet. "Do you want the one with the blue shirt or the one with the orange shirt? Chase or Dean?"

"Wow, you guys are picky," Spencer commented drily. "I thought you only dated guys with red shirts."

I raised my eyebrows and looked at him wearing a Ben & Jerry's ice-cream T-shirt. "Well, I don't know, but green shirts are definitely out of the question."

"Ouch. Ouch!" Adam pretended to dab

blood from Spencer's nose.

We were arguing about whether it was ethical to invite people to a party that wasn't yours when our parents marched up. My mother stared at me. "Ice cream? Honey, you'll ruin your lunch."

"It's not ice cream. It's sherbet," I said.

"But we're going to Awful Arthur's. Home of the Happy Oyster," she said.

"Well, then. Forget this," I said, tossing my nearly empty container into a trash can. "Not that I like oysters or have ever tried one or wanted to try one."

"Is it true what they say about oysters?" Spencer asked.

"What?" My mother put her hand on her throat. "I don't know what you're referring to."

"They're supposed to have an aphrodisiac effect," said Spencer. "Do they?"

Heather stared at him, then scrunched up her face. "You mean they make you afraid to leave the house?"

"No, that's agoraphobic," Spencer said as we all laughed.

"Let me get this straight. You got into Linden, and I didn't," Adam said to Heather. "Really?"

"You know how they want a very diverse student body," Heather said. "Well, I'm diverse."

"As diverse as they get," Spencer muttered.

"So what *does* it mean?" Heather asked.

"It means we should be going," my mother said as she opened the van's side door. "Quickly. Climb in, everyone!"

Spencer got into the van. "Heather, it means that eating oysters makes you have certain thoughts. About members of the opposite sex."

"*Really*. Interesting," she commented. "Maybe we should look into that."

I felt myself blushing at the very suggestion as I sat in the second row back.

"Maybe *you* don't need to, Heather," Adam said, laughing as he dropped into the spot beside her.

"Hey, I saw you checking out that girl in the gift shop—" Heather began.

"Me? I was not."

"Yeah, she was too busy asking for my number," said Spencer, tapping his cell phone in front of my face as if that proved anything.

"Oh, right. You?" I scoffed.

"Why not me?" he said. Our eyes met, and he—unlike me—didn't seem uncomfortable at all. On the one hand, I was glad he'd forgotten our encounter—on the other hand, I hated that he had. Was he so arrogant that he'd just brushed aside the incident as a harmless crush? And how had I ever had a crush on *him*?

"Check it out." Spencer started to show us a picture on his phone.

"Who's that?" I asked.

"Oh. That's my neighbor's dog at home. She just had puppies, so . . ."

We all laughed.

"I knew you were making up that gift-shop girl story," Adam said to him. "Since when has anyone ever asked for your number?"

"All the time," Spencer replied. "Constantly. Just like you're constantly going out," he said to me.

Touché, I thought. "Yeah, well, you take

really bad pictures," I said, looking at his phone. "Of cute puppies."

"It's a phone," he said, snapping it closed.

After lunch, the four of us gathered on the beach outside the house. Adam hadn't stopped trying to convince us to play a sport—any kind of sport, he pleaded desperately, as if he were suffering withdrawal being around us.

"Two-on-two, come on," he urged. "Just like beach volleyball in the Olympics."

"All right, fine," Heather sighed. "But you're being really obnoxious."

"And you're bound to be disappointed because I'm not very good at this, okay? And by 'not very good,' I mean, the last time I played I was probably a foot shorter," I said.

"Come on, just try for fifteen minutes," Adam said. "If you hate it, we'll stop and . . . I don't know. Play cards or something."

Spencer tossed the ball to me. "Look at it this way, Em. If the next-door Neanderthals can play it—"

"You haven't even talked to them," I said.

"How can you insult them?"

"It's easy. They're a type."

"You're a type. A really judgmental and rude type." I tossed the ball into the air and took a whack with my fist. I ended up spiking the ball, and it slammed into the sand right beside Adam, who jumped.

"Did you see her vertical leap?" He stood back in amazement. "You should have been playing basketball all these years, not ballet."

Spencer stared at me. "Were you aiming at me? Because you missed."

"I call Emily for my team. In perpetuity," Adam said.

"Purple what?" asked Heather.

"He means forever. For all time," I explained.

"Adam. I didn't know you felt that way about Emily," Heather teased.

"Shut up. It's a game. I care about winning," Adam said. "Now get over there and play."

I found myself wishing that Blake and his

friends would see us and come out, to prove Spencer wrong. Apparently Heather had the same thought, because she said, "Hold on a second, let's see if we can get some more players. Come on, Emily—come with me!"

"Great idea," I said, joining her. We ran up to the steps to their deck and looked around for Blake, Trevor, and the other guys. The place looked deserted. We went down to the pool on the bottom level, and even knocked on the back door.

"Not home. Too bad," she said.

"It was still a good idea. Except then they'd have to see me play," I said.

"You wouldn't have to actually play, just pretend while you made small talk," Heather said.

"Oh, is that how you do it?" I teased her, and we jumped off the bottom step back onto the beach.

"So? Are they coming?" asked Adam, looking impatient.

"Nope. Not home," Heather announced.

"Probably out riding dune buggies and Jet Skis and trampling the earth," Spencer commented.

"Yeah, okay, Al Gore. Or maybe they're on a walk," I said.

"I'm just saying—did you see how much trash they left on the deck?" Spencer asked.

"They're probably separating stuff for recycling," I said.

"Come on, you don't really think—"

"Quit stalling, Spence," Adam interrupted. "Are we here to argue or to play?" He launched the volleyball across the net, and his serve nearly popped Spencer in the face.

"Game *on!*" Spencer said as he managed to get it back across the net to me.

As I leaped for the ball, I thought, *Please don't let Blake come back right when I do something incredibly stupid. Please!*

Before getting into bed that night, I walked out onto the tiny balcony just outside my bedroom. I didn't see or hear much of anything from Blake's house, but the moon was amazing. It wasn't a full moon, but it was close—maybe a day or two away. I went back inside to get my camera and tried to get some shots of it.

I'd taken a few photos when I heard some guys talking. I looked down below and saw Blake, Trevor, and some other guys heading across the parking lot, in the direction of the main drag.

"There goes your friend," a voice suddenly said in the darkness.

"Ack!" I let out a little scream—or maybe it was a big scream—as I nearly toppled over the edge of the balcony's railing.

Blake and Trevor turned around and peered back at the house, trying to see where the dying-animal noise had come from. I stepped into the shadow as much as I could, but also gave a pathetic friendly wave, in case they could see me. Thankfully, they didn't seem to notice me, and they turned around and kept walking, heading toward town.

Spencer leaned over the balcony that was diagonally downstairs from mine and peered up at me. "Good evening," he said in a creepy, fake-Dracula voice.

"That was you? Don't do that."

"What?"

"Embarrass me like that," I said. "How did you know I was out here?"

"I heard your door slide open. Light emerged. Et cetera."

"Well, next time give me some warning or something!" I pleaded.

"Oh, sure. I'll just yell, 'Hi, Emily, what are you doing out here, are you looking for the guys next door, because they're right there!' Or, you know, something like that."

If I'd had anything to throw at him, besides my camera and a plastic deck chair, I would have. "What were you doing out here, anyway?" I asked as I sat down and propped my feet on the railing.

"Oh. Well, I was thinking of sleeping out here." He leaned on the railing, looking up at me.

"Really? Isn't it kind of hot?" A couple of motorcycles accelerated from a stop sign out on the road. "And occasionally loud?" I asked.

"I want some privacy," he said. "My parents and I have a suite. So even though I have my own room, I kind of don't have my own room. You know what I mean?"

I tried to picture the layout of the room. "Not exactly."

"I'll show you tomorrow," he said. "Let's just say that the concept of *suite* is not exactly *sweet*. How did you get so lucky to score your own room?"

"We got here before you?" I guessed.

"Remind me to change the rules for the next trip. We'll draw straws," he said. "And I'll cut the straws, and I'll go first."

"That's exactly what I'd expect from you," I said.

"What's that supposed to mean?"

"Nothing. So what are you doing, reading by the light of the moon?" I asked.

"That, and some streetlights and a book-light. Kurt Vonnegut. Ever read anything by him?"

"No, I don't think so," I said.

"Really?"

"Yes, really."

"I'm just surprised. I mean, you go to a fairly decent school, right?"

"It was a great school, one of the top ones in the district," I said, defending the place that I'd complained about for four years straight. You found yourself doing strange things when you were insulted, when your West Side Lions pride was at stake.

"So what are you planning to major in?"

"I don't know. I want to leave myself open and be flexible. Photography, maybe?" I said.

"Photography. Huh. Can you actually major in that?"

"Why not?"

"Seems kind of lightweight."

I didn't know if I could do some kind of Spider-Man move and swing down to his balcony and kick him in the teeth, but I was tempted to try. "Do you really need to put me down? You always have to get your digs in, like you're so much better than the rest of us."

"Sorry!" Spencer laughed.

"It's not funny."

"I didn't know you were so thin-skinned," Spencer said.

"I'm not. *You're* so rude and arrogant." I pushed back my chair and stood up, wondering if it was too late to follow Blake and his pals into town. That sounded a lot more fun than hanging out here, getting insulted by Spencer.

"Come on, Em, I was only—"

"And I'm only going inside," I said, sliding the door closed behind me.

Some people had changed more over the years than you expected them to, and some people hadn't changed at all.

Chapter 6

*T*he next morning I managed to get up very early and took some gorgeous photos of the sunrise over the ocean. I was hoping that Blake would wake up early, too, see me out on the beach, and feel compelled to come join me. It could be just like in my dream. Sure, why not? He'd run out, call my name . . . I'd run toward him and jump into his waiting arms, and he'd twirl me around, the way in-love couples were supposed to do.

But no, the only being that had approached me so far was a seagull—a very aggressive seagull, who'd nearly made off with my break-fast bar. He'd twirled around me for about five minutes before giving up. That was the only twirling going on this morning.

I lay down on my towel and stretched my arms above my head, then I rolled over onto my stomach and rested my cheek against my arms. I was so relaxed that I was nearly ready to go back to sleep. Maybe it was time for me to go get another cup of coffee, I thought. Or maybe I should just give in: After all, this *was* my vacation, and maybe Blake would see me sleeping out here and decide to . . . I don't know . . . snuggle up against me because—

Suddenly, I heard someone clearing their throat.

I looked up just in time to see Blake drop onto the sand beside me. "Morning," he said. "Did I wake you up?"

"N-no," I said as I turned over to sit beside him. He was wearing long, madras plaid shorts, a bright yellow polo shirt, a white cap, and no shoes. Something about his getup didn't quite add up, but I didn't say anything.

"Nice day," Blake commented. He held out a white bag. "Here. We stopped by the bakery on the way home last night. There were thirteen to start with. I think. Have one," he offered.

"Thanks," I said, gently pulling a powdered doughnut out of the bag. "I think I saw you guys leave last night, when I was out on my balcony."

Blake snapped his fingers against my bare leg. "Was that you who shrieked?"

Oops, forgot that part. "You heard me? Well, I kind of slipped and lost my balance—no big whoop."

"You almost plummeted to your death. No big whoop," he teased. "Y'all are crazy."

"Anyway, what did you guys do?"

"Oh, we went into town to see if we could find something to do. We didn't. But we did find out about a band coming in a couple days. They're great—I've seen them play before."

"Yeah?"

"Yeah. We'll have to go," he said.

Was he asking me out? I'd hardly ever been asked out before, so I wasn't sure. Did "we'll have to go" count as a date? "Definitely," I said.

"Look out, you've got some powdered sugar

right there." He brushed at my arm, and I felt a shiver go up my spine. "You have a great body. You know that? I mean, you probably know that. Never mind."

I knew that by this point, my entire upper torso must be blushing. I was used to having ballet instructors comment on my line—not guys comment on my curves. "I do? I mean . . . thanks."

"You do sports? Work out?"

"I dance," I said.

He shot me a questioning look.

"Ballet," I explained.

"Isn't that kind of expensive? Don't you have to starve yourself?"

"Yes, and no." I held up the doughnut, and we both laughed.

"What did you guys do yesterday?" Blake asked. "I looked around for you a couple of times but you weren't around."

He'd looked around for me? Why did I have to be touring lighthouses? Mom and her plans. Her wicked plans. "We, uh, we saw lots of things. We were basically stuck in a van with our parents for the whole day," I admitted, hating to seem young. "Today we're going to see if we can, you know, do something without them." *Unless I get a better offer, that is.* "What are you up to?" I asked.

"Us? We're off to play golf again."

"Barefoot?" I asked. *Who do you think you are, Spencer?* I almost added. And was the fact they had something in common a bad thing?

"My golf spikes are in the car. You only wear them on the green."

"Right. Of course. Well, then that makes sense, I guess." Open mouth, insert sand-covered foot.

Blake glanced at his watch. "I should get going."

"Yeah, me too, probably."

We both got to our feet, and I was about to ask him if he maybe wanted to teach me how to golf when Heather and Spencer came outside. Heather grinned when she saw me standing with Blake—me in my bikini and long T-shirt, and Blake in his golfing clothes.

"Well. *Good* morning," she said, walking up to us.

"Hey, y'all," Blake said. "Doughnut?" He held out the bag to Spencer. "We got them late last night, but they're still really fresh."

Heather's smile widened. "You guys have been out here eating doughnuts all night?"

Spencer looked slightly horrified by the thought as he pulled a chocolate doughnut out of the bag, as if the idea of me and Blake eating a baker's dozen tainted his breakfast somehow.

"No, not *all* night." Blake laughed. "I just came out and found her here."

"Funny. It's almost like she was waiting for you," Spencer said.

"I was taking pictures," I said through gritted teeth. I wanted to get Blake's golf clubs from the car and whack Spencer in the head with them.

He was just happily munching on the chocolate doughnut, like he hadn't suggested a thing.

"Actually, more like sleeping, when I saw you," Blake said.

"She needs to rest between pictures. Very

exhausting work, photography," Spencer said.

I glared at him. "You have no idea."

"Anyway, we've got great news, kiddo," Spencer said, after taking another big bite of doughnut and polishing off the whole thing.

"I'm not a k-kiddo," I managed to stammer, despite the fact I was feeling like a kid with a crush. On Blake. I couldn't believe I'd ever had a crush on Spencer.

"We found three bikes in the shed beside the house—we're planning a trip down the coast," Spencer said. "There's enough for all four of us—one of the bikes is a tandem."

I glanced at Heather. Did we necessarily want to spend the whole day with Adam and Spencer?

"You guys have fun," Blake said. "I have to get going or I'll miss tee-time. See you tonight?" he called over his shoulder as he headed off the beach toward the parking lot.

"I don't know," said Heather. "I'm not sure."

He stopped walking and faced us. "Oh, come on, you've got to be there."

She laughed. "I was just kidding. Of course we'll be there!" she said.

"Oh, yeah, you won't get rid of them," Spencer said. "You'll try, like we've tried, but still, no. They're like—"

"We're *going* now," Heather said, dragging Spencer away by force.

"Okay, so . . . how did you convince our parents to let us go exploring on our own?" I asked.

"They're going to play golf too, and they couldn't see any reason to drag us along when none of us actually play," he said.

Well, no, but, um . . . If we were to happen to go to the same golf course as Blake and everyone, wouldn't that be kind of a nice coincidence? "We could learn," I suggested.

"Run around hitting a tiny ball wearing plaid shorts?" Spencer shook his head. "I don't think so."

"What are you talking about? I love the plaid shorts," said Heather.

"Me too," I said. *Especially on certain people.*

Spencer stared at both of us and let out a

long sigh. "Well, you guys can golf. I'm going to explore the Outer Banks and try to make something out of this vacation. Emily, what are you waiting for? Where's your camera?" he asked.

"Right here. Why?"

"Don't you want to get a picture of that?" he asked.

"Of what?" I replied.

Spencer held out his hands as if he were framing a picture. "Volleyball dude driving away. Car vanishing. Taillights. Turn signal. Et cetera."

I laughed and shook my head. "You have no artistic sense."

"Oh, sure. It's *me* without the artistic sense," he scoffed.

"What, are you saying I don't have any?" I could have smacked him with my camera for saying that, except I valued it more than I valued Spencer at the moment. It might break on his hard, stubborn head.

"I'm just saying that your subjects are kind of limited so far," he commented.

I glared at him. "So is your imagination.

How would you know what I photograph and what I don't? Are you psychic now in addition to being older, smarter—"

"All right, kids. Do I have to separate you?" Heather asked.

"Let's just say we won't be the ones riding the tandem bike," Spencer said as he walked into the house.

"Works for me!" I called after him.

After a lot of discussion, we'd decided to head out on the bikes to find a different beach to hang out at. Heather and Adam were managing to stay well ahead of us on the tandem bike, while Spencer and I were riding in single file. I didn't know how—or why—he managed to ride barefoot, but he did.

We'd talked Heather out of riding bikes up to Corolla in search of the lighthouse guys, since we'd already sort of seen the area. We'd headed south.

Finally Adam and Heather stopped at the entrance to a beautiful, sandy beach. "You guys, let's stop here and hang out," Adam said when we caught up.

I took off my helmet and brushed a damp strand of hair off my forehead. "Sounds good to me."

"Then maybe we can find a place to go windsurfing," Spencer said as we locked our bikes to the rack in the parking lot.

"Oh, yeah, we'll do that, we'll totally do that," I said, grabbing the towel I'd fastened onto the back of the bike.

Heather laughed. "Can you picture me on a windsurfer? I'm too short. I'd get knocked down."

"Not necessarily," Adam said. "It's all about balance, which you're good at. But you need upper body strength, too."

"Can I have some of yours?" asked Heather as we traipsed onto the beach.

I watched Adam and Spencer strip off their shirts and dive into the ocean. Heather was wearing a bikini under her T-shirt and shorts, and she stripped down and followed them.

I took out my camera and took pictures of the long beach, the rolling surf, and the trail of clothes leading to the water. There were a few small children farther down the beach playing in the water and building sand castles, and I tried to get good photos of them, too. I put my camera away, stashing it inside my shorts pocket and covering those with a towel.

"What are you waiting for?" Spencer called to me from the surf.

I stood there, water up to my ankles. Then my lower shins. Then my mid-shins. Then my knees.

Spencer swam a little closer. "What's the matter? Are you scared?"

"No, I'm not scared," I said. "I like to think of it as smart, actually."

His arms cut through the water as he made his way toward shore. He didn't have the same gigantic biceps that Adam had, but he was definitely in good shape. Just not the same weight-lifter look. "How do you figure?"

I wrapped my arms around my waist. "It's freezing! Why would I want to go all the way in?"

"Because the water feels great once you're

in. But hey, if you want to stand there and shiver, feel free." He stood up and pointed. "We'll head out past the break, float for a while."

He turned to swim back out. I didn't want to go in, but I didn't want to be the only one who didn't, either. "But I—I can't just leave my camera here, without anyone watching it."

"No one's going to take it. Do you even see anyone else around? That's not it. You're afraid of seaweed or jellyfish or something," he teased.

"No, I'm not!" Although, come to think of it, I didn't like slimy, gel-like stinging creatures floating past me in the ocean. "Well, maybe. Have you seen any?"

"Come on, live dangerously for once. Do something not on your mom's list."

I slowly tiptoed farther into the water until it came up to my waist. "Since when do I not live dangerously? I mean, I'm here with you, right?"

"You are *so* going under." Spencer struggled to get close enough to push me into the ocean, but before he could, someone else pulled my leg out from under me and I went straight down into the water.

I came to the surface and saw Heather standing behind me, laughing. "Sometimes you just have to give Emily a little push," she said to Spencer, who was laughing.

"Oh, my God, you should have seen your face," he said.

I glared at both of them, then dove under an approaching wave and escaped out to calmer water by myself. I floated for a minute or two, looking up at the deep blue sky. It was very peaceful, and I felt myself getting lost in my thoughts as I gently bobbed in the waves. I was so lucky to be here, lucky to have this vacation with my family and friends.

I didn't want to get too deep—either in thought or in the ocean—but I couldn't help thinking that this was some sort of turning point, between high school and college. It wasn't just that it was the last summer before college, and not that I was one to make swimming metaphors . . . but I felt like I was on a diving board, about to plunge into a new life. Sort of like how I'd stood in the water just five minutes ago. Wasn't I ready to take more risks than that? Did I have to stand there and wait? Couldn't I just jump right in, like everyone else?

Maybe it was time to start doing things first, and worrying about them later.

"So." Heather swam over to me while I was contemplating how I could change my life. "What time are we going to go over to Blake's tonight, and what are you going to wear?"

I appreciate friends who can keep things in perspective.

We got out of the water after swimming for about twenty minutes. I felt like a prune. A very cold prune.

"You might have given up ballet, but you still have ballet belly," Adam commented as we walked up toward where we'd left our outer layers.

I laughed. "What's ballet belly?"

"No belly. A complete lack of belly."

I felt myself turn red. "Oh. Thanks. I guess."

You know how sometimes when certain people make comments, you really aren't sure if it's a compliment or not? That's how it was with Spencer and Adam. They were so used to teasing me and Heather, making fun of us, that you couldn't take anything they said seriously. They'd always follow it up with a quip about something we were doing wrong.

Then again, we weren't exactly kind to them, either. Over the years we'd learned to give back as good as we got.

Adam spread out a large T-shirt on the sand and sat on it, while Heather unfolded a beach towel. I grabbed the towel from where I'd tossed it in the sand, being careful to take out my camera first and place it carefully on top of my tank top.

Spencer dropped right onto the sand, soaking wet. "You look almost blue." He reached out and touched my arm. "You know what it is?

You've got that ballerina skin. Gets cold faster."

"I know, I'm pale and—look, would everyone quit with the ballerina comments already? I'm not a ballerina!" I laughed, but I was serious. You know the expression, beating a dead horse? This was the same thing. It hadn't even been all that funny—or true—the first time.

"Maybe you just have thin skin," Adam said.

"Ballerinas don't have thin skin and neither do I," I said.

"Could have fooled me," Spencer commented.

I turned over and buried my face in the towel, wishing that everyone would stop talking about me. I was so tired and sleepy from getting up early that morning, and the sun felt so warm and nice . . . I could almost fall asleep, right here. In fact, I should.

"Let's not just sit around," Adam said. "Let's do something. I know—I stashed a Wiffle Ball and bat in my bike bag—I'll go get it and we can play Wiffle Ball."

"How about playing the napping game?"

I mumbled into my towel.

"How about the game where we find a beach with other people on it?" Heather asked. "I'll go with you, Adam. I left my bike bottle on the bike and I need some water."

Spencer sifted grains of sand onto the back of my feet while they were gone. "Come on, get up."

"Why?" I muttered, still facing the sand.

"You know Adam—you have to play Wiffle Ball whether you want to or not. Besides, if you just lie here, facedown, you'll miss something else. I'm not sure what, but something. And everyone at home will ask how your amazing Outer Banks vacation was, and you'll have to say, 'Um, I slept through it.' Then you'll get to Linden and everyone will have to sit around in a circle during orientation and talk about their summer. Everyone will be bragging about canoe trips and mountaineering and NBA basketball camp—"

"How do you know all this?"

"I've, you know. Talked to friends. I've heard that's what they do," Spencer said.

"Oh."

"You won't have anything meaningful to say. You'll start yawning, thinking about this trip."

I sat up and rubbed the side of my face. "Well, whose fault would *that* be?" I readjusted myself so I was comfortably facing the ocean, and leaned back on my elbows.

"Yours. Totally yours," Spencer said. "And if I have to sit near you at any point during fresh-person orientation, I will disavow any and all knowledge of this trip."

"Oh, me too. It'll be like we never met," I said.

Are we flirting? I wondered. *I think we're flirting. Why isn't Heather here to tell me? Or, better yet, to STOP me?*

I'd never told her about how I'd pined for Spencer that last trip, how I was convinced we were meant for each other.

Thank goodness only two of us had to be embarrassed for me on that account: me and Spencer. This was almost the first time we'd been alone so far this trip (not counting our balcony argument), and I was expecting it to be dreadfully awkward. But so far, it wasn't bad.

We sat and watched the water for a minute. In the distance I could see a large freighter that appeared to be moving at a snail's pace. I watched as the waves rolled onto the sand, the water bubbles foaming and then popping. "Why is being near the ocean so relaxing? I could sit here all day," I mused. "Tide coming in—"

"Actually, it's going out," Spencer said. "See how the dark line where the water ends is going down?"

"Oh. Well, whatever," I said. He always had to be right.

"So, do you spend a lot of time at the ocean? I mean, did you, um, go anywhere on spring break this year?"

"No, my parents didn't want me to," I said.

"You've been sheltered. Overprotective 'rents."

"Exactly. I think we've already established that."

"You should have gone to New Orleans," Spencer went on.

What did he mean? With him? To see him?

"Because," he continued, "the area could use more volunteers. But most people our age are too busy watching TV—"

"I volunteer plenty," I said. "I teach beginning dance and stretching classes for seniors at a retirement home. I organized a dance marathon at school that raised money for Special Olympics. Plus, I'm in a troupe that performs for hospital fund-raisers. So don't assume so much about other people, okay?"

"Okay." Spencer looked momentarily at a loss for words. "Sorry, Mother Teresa."

I jumped up as Adam and Heather returned, carrying the long, skinny bat and white plastic ball.

"I want Mother Teresa on my side," Heather said as Adam started to create a diamond, using clumps of dried seaweed for the bases. "Girls versus boys."

"Really?" Spencer asked. "Don't you think . . . um . . ."

"No, I don't. Really, I want to be on Emily's

team. She kicked your butt in volleyball, didn't she?" Heather reminded him.

"Did I mention I haven't played Wiffle Ball in about three years?" I said as I took position at home plate, the bat resting on my shoulder. This wasn't going to be pretty.

Adam lobbed the first pitch to me, and I took a swing at it and missed. I tossed the ball back toward him, but it only made it halfway. "You sure you want to play?" I asked as we went through the same routine three more times.

"Come on, you'll get it this time," Heather said. "Don't give up."

I concentrated as hard as I could, took a big swing, and knocked the ball over to the left, past Adam, just as Heather's cell rang and she answered it. I was so shocked by the fact I'd gotten a hit that I stood there for a second without moving. Then I bolted for first base. I hit the seaweed base and turned to keep going, but my foot sank into the sand at a weird angle, and I yelped. It felt like I'd twisted my ankle. I hopped up and down while Spencer ran over to tag me out.

"I know you don't know much about base-ball, but you're supposed to keep going," he said. "What dance is that?" he asked.

"The leave me alone hop," I grunted. "This kills."

"Spencer, help her already!" Heather cried. She was talking on her cell phone.

"I think I sprained my ankle," I told him as he put his arm around my waist to steady me, and guided me to a sitting position.

"Is it really sprained?" Spencer asked. "Because I'd hate Wiffle Ball to be the cause of you giving up your dance career—oops." He snapped his fingers. "You already did that."

I laughed, despite the fact my ankle was throbbing uncomfortably. "It wasn't a dance career," I said. "Think of it as my sport. Like how you played . . . wait a second. What *did* you play?"

"Lacrosse," he said. "Badly. So. How does it feel now? You know, I could take a look. I've twisted my ankle a dozen times."

"Fine. I guess." I heard Heather shrieking and looked over to see her and Adam chasing after the Wiffle Ball, which was blowing away down the beach.

Spencer put his hand on my ankle and gently pressed all sides of it. I winced, but more from the fact he was touching me again and sort of giving me a massage than from the fact that it did sort of feel like my ankle was swelling. I'd had serious ankle injuries before, too, and this didn't feel like one of them. But I hadn't ever had a cute boy treat them before, either.

Cute boy? What am I saying? This is Spencer.

Anyway, even if he is sort of cute, I can't like Spencer again, I thought. I didn't get it. How could I still be physically attracted to someone so rude and arrogant? Didn't my brain try to screen out these things?

But I had a feeling my brain was on vacation, like me, when it came to that sort of thing. My brain was not involved.

"You know what? I'll be okay," I said. "It doesn't hurt as much anymore."

"You sure?"

I nodded. "I'll just rest it for a while before we pedal home. But maybe you should help them—they look clueless." I pointed at Heather and Adam who were standing onshore helplessly watching the ball go out with the tide.

Spencer shrugged, slowly letting go of my foot. "It's only a Wiffle Ball. We can buy another."

"Spencer, do your Al Gore thing. Think of the environment. Birds could choke on that."

"You're right!" He jumped up, ran off, and dove into the water, leaving me sitting there to contemplate what had just happened.

Chapter 7

"*N*o, don't worry, you look fantastic. Only, how about we do this?" Heather made a last-minute adjustment to my hair, un-clipping the barrette and letting my hair fan out over my shoulders.

"Really?" I asked.

"Really. God, I'd kill for your hair. Show it off," she said.

I ran my fingers through my hair, combing it a bit. "I guess I'm just more used to having it held back."

"The ballet and gymnastics years. I know. It took me months to stop doing that," she said.

"Do you miss it?" I asked.

"What? The hairstyle?"

"No, the gymnastics," I said.

"Sure. Of course, who wouldn't?"

"Do you think maybe you'll get back into it sometime? At Linden, maybe?"

"There's a club, so I'll check it out—it wouldn't hurt to try. Plus, it's always a good way to meet people, make friends. But it sort of seems like—that was my former life. As a kid. You know? I couldn't go back even if I wanted to. In some ways, I do want to, but . . . anyway. What about you?"

"I guess I'll still dance. I'll just try other things, too," I said.

"Like partying," Heather said.

I laughed. "Well. I wasn't exactly thinking *that*."

"Come on, get with the program. You know what? Maybe those guys from Kur-ulla will call soon, too. We might end up staying out late. Are we ready for that?" asked Heather.

I shrugged, wondering what else I could do to prepare myself. "Ready as we'll ever be, I guess."

"Oh, come on, you can do better than that.

How about some enthusiasm?"

I frowned. "You sound like my mother."

Heather clapped her hand over her mouth. "Forgive me," she whispered through her fingers. "That was definitely not my intention."

We headed outside without inviting Adam and Spencer to come along at the same time. If they decided to show up, too, that was fine, but we didn't want to walk in the door and appear to be "with" them. That would ruin everything.

"Do you think they'll think we're too young?" I asked as we walked around the back of our house to theirs.

"Does who think that?" Heather asked.

"Blake and Trevor," I said in a soft voice. "I mean, they could be twenty, or twenty-one, even." Somehow, the prospect of my first fling being with someone that much older than me seemed a little unlikely. Not to mention a bit off-putting, in some way.

We stopped outside the door, and I heard music coming from inside.

"Eighteen-year-olds go out with twenty-one-year-olds all the time," Heather said.

"What are you talking about?"

I'm talking about a totally inexperienced eighteen-year-old, I thought. Except I wasn't talking. Just thinking. And maybe, sort of, worrying. The way I was acting around Blake, flirting and all—that really wasn't me. That was just a part I was playing, trying to keep up with Heather.

I don't know the first thing about actually hooking up with someone, I thought as we walked in and I saw Blake standing by the kitchen counter, talking to several other guys.

The house next door seemed to have the exact same layout as our rental. A couple dozen people were hanging out on the first floor, sitting at the kitchen's long, tall counter or playing pool or lounging on the comfy living room chairs. "How do they know so many people?" I asked Heather as we edged into the room.

"They're popular?" she suggested. "Which is never a bad quality. Or, you know, *almost* never."

"Hey! You guys came!" Blake greeted us with a big smile. He seemed genuinely happy to see us.

"Sure, of course we did," said Heather. "Nice place. Looks kind of familiar. How long are you guys staying here, anyway?"

"A few weeks. My family owns this," Trevor said. "My extended family, I should have said—my parents, aunts and uncles, grandparents. We split up the time between families—my folks and a couple of their friends will be here next week, so it's not going to be as much fun," Trevor explained. "That's why we need to have all the parties *now*."

I nodded. "Good idea."

"Or, how about this: Maybe we could get *all* the sets of parents to share one house and we could share the other," Heather suggested.

"Oh, yeah. They'd go for that." Trevor shook his head and laughed. "How about if you suggest it? They might take it better, coming from you."

"Be careful. She can talk people into anything," I warned him.

"These guys are from Wisconsin. Staying next door," Blake told the rest of the group.

"Wisconsin, huh? Have you defrosted yet?" asked one of his friends.

"Actually, I was thinking that it's kind of hot in here," said Heather.

"Yeah. We're fine. It's not that cold. *All* the time," I said.

We made small talk with different people and played a bad game of pool with two other girls, which took us at least half an hour. I managed to sink a couple of striped balls by accident, which would have been good if Heather and I weren't supposed to knock in the solid ones.

At one point I spotted Adam across the room. Where was Spencer? I wondered. Was he that antisocial? And then I remembered that I didn't care about Spencer and he could take care of himself, anyway. If he wanted to sit inside and read all night, and be surrounded by parents greedy for every last detail of his personal life, then so be it.

"Hey, where've you been?" asked Blake.

"Losing. Badly."

"Billiards aren't your thing?"

"No. And pool's not, either." We both laughed.

"Beach volleyball?"

I wrinkled my nose. "Mmm . . . not so much."

"That's okay." He put his arm around my shoulder and squeezed. "You know what? I'm really glad you decided to spend your vacation here."

"Well, I don't know if I decided anything, but me too," I said. "I mean, same goes for me. And you."

Blake laughed. "I think I know what you mean."

"Well, that makes *one* of us." I rolled my eyes. I didn't know what I was saying, but I did realize that it didn't make much sense.

"It's such a coincidence that you'd be here," Blake went on.

I laughed. "You invited me!"

"No," he said, putting his hand on my arm. "Not *here*, tonight. I mean, here, next door."

"Oh. Right. Um, how so?"

"Well, because we wouldn't have met. Usually you end up at these places, and you could be staying next to anybody. Could be some old people. Some young brats. Or snobs, or people who tell you to turn down the music all the time. That ruins everything."

"Right." I nodded.

"So instead, you're here. It's so awesome."

There was an awkward pause. I tried to think of something to say. It wasn't easy. Then I remembered something. "You know what? I got the best pictures of you guys from earlier today."

"You did? When?"

"You were on your boogie boards, surfing. Hold on, I'll show you." I reached into my shorts pocket. Cell phone—check. Camera? No check. "I can't believe it. I forgot my camera."

"Oh, well, I'll see 'em another time."

"No, I mean, this is really weird for me. I take it *everywhere*," I said. "I think I'd better go check my room to make sure I didn't lose it." That would be a nightmare. Without my computer here, I hadn't had a chance to back things up.

"I'll come with you," Blake offered. "Sometimes it helps to have another person look."

"Oh? Right. But, um, do you really think you should leave your own party?" I asked, suddenly feeling nervous about the prospect of being alone with Blake.

"It's only for a few minutes. Right?"

"Right," I said.

"We'll get your camera and come right back," he said.

"We'd have to," I said. "Otherwise everyone would miss us."

"Well, I don't know about *that*." Blake laughed.

On our way outside, I saw Spencer and Adam talking to a couple of girls in the kitchen, while they helped themselves to chips and soda. So Spencer had made it after all. I waved at Heather, who was perched on a stool by the pool table, watching the latest game.

Blake followed me up the four flights of stairs. "You're way up here? Cool," he commented. "You have privacy."

"You'd think so," I said as I opened the door. "So, um, this is my room. Now, about that camera . . ."

"You get a balcony, too? Cool."

"Ah! Here it is." I picked up my camera from my bed, where I'd left it and followed him out onto the balcony. In the dark, I clicked through photos, trying to locate the ones of Blake from that afternoon.

Blake leaned over my shoulder to look at the display screen. "Hold on, I can't see anything." He pushed back my hair so that it fell over my shoulder and wasn't in his way. Then he put his hands on my waist and pulled me back toward him so I was leaning against him, and vice versa. "Okay, start the slide show."

I'd never stood so close to a guy before, let alone someone as good-looking as Blake, let alone someone that good-looking who I was kind of interested in. It was all I could do to remember how the camera operated.

All of a sudden, I heard a door slide open. I wondered which room it belonged to, and tried to ignore it.

Blake laughed as we scrolled through a shot where he wiped out on a wave. "Okay, y'all are not allowed to take any more pictures of me falling on my face."

"The camera doesn't judge," I told him.

"Emily?"

I looked down and saw Spencer, who I had *just* seen at the party, leaning over his balcony railing, looking up at us.

"I didn't know you guys were out here," he said.

"Well, we are," I said as Blake slowly released my waist. Was Spencer trying to ruin this moment for me?

"You guys hear about the storm that's coming?" Spencer said.

"No," I said through gritted teeth.

"What storm?" asked Blake.

"Supposed to be major. Strong winds. Hurricane-like," Spencer said.

"When?" I asked.

"Not sure exactly. They're talking about it making landfall sometime tomorrow."

Are we really out here discussing the weather, when I could—and should—rightfully be kissing Blake? "I didn't hear anything about a big storm," I said.

"Oh, it's all over the news. Tropical storm Brittany."

"I thought only hurricanes had women's names," Blake commented.

"Anyway. Well, you guys, uh—see you back at the party! Oh, and Emily—your dad was looking for you. He might be on his way up, actually."

Blake coughed and took a step back into the room. "You know what? I should get back to the party."

"Really?"

He made a beeline for the door. "Really. Like I said, I probably shouldn't leave my own party."

You didn't say that! I wanted to call after him as he disappeared down the staircase. *I said that! And I take it back!*

I stood there at the top of the steps, half fuming and half relieved. Fuming was winning.

Two minutes later, Spencer's mother opened the door, with a mud mask covering her face. His dad was lying on the bed, his back propped on pillows, watching TV. He waved hello.

"Emily! What's up?" Mrs. Flanagan asked. "Everything okay?"

"Sure."

"Really? You look a little flushed," she commented.

I put my hand to my cheek. "It's the sun. Lots of time in the sun."

"Be careful with that. You could do a mud mask with me. Or would you like some moisturizer? I have some excellent organic tea tree oil and coconut—"

"Thanks, but no thanks. Excuse me. I need to see Spencer."

"Oh, okay. I should have known, right? Have we told you yet how happy we are that you'll be at school together?"

Only about a hundred times. "I'm happy, too," I told her with a smile. *Just absolutely thrilled to pieces.*

She smiled and gestured toward a side door. "He's right in there. Got back a few minutes ago."

"Emily, how's it going?" Mr. Flanagan asked as I walked past him.

"Just great," I said. *If it weren't for your annoying son, it might be . . . going. Somewhere.*

I knocked on the door, heard Spencer call "Enter!" and slipped inside. His bed took up most of the room. His clothes lying all over the floor took up the rest of it. He was sitting in a small wicker chair by the door to the balcony.

"I see what you mean."

"What?"

"About the suite thing." For a second, I forgot my mission. I looked at all the stuff in his room, making my way across the T-shirt-covered floor to where he sat—not that I needed to be any closer to talk to him. "I didn't even know you *brought* this many clothes."

"So, did the party, um, break up?" he asked without making eye contact.

"Right. That's why I came to see you. What was *that* all about?"

"What? It *is* windy. I just thought—"

"You just thought you'd interrupt my night with a fake storm, that's what. And just because you sacrificed your nonexistent social life to help out after a hurricane—which I totally admire by the way and I wish I didn't right now—we're supposed to believe you when you invent stories about tropical storms, which isn't even funny, and you should know it isn't funny, because after all you saw the damage first-hand—"

"Whoa, whoa! Take a breath, why don't you?" Spencer said, laughing, kicking back, looking completely relaxed, while I fumed on.

"It comes down to this," I said. "You pretty much ruined my night. You were at the party, then we left, then the next thing I know you're back here—*checking* on us?"

"I got bored at the party. There wasn't anyone to talk to."

I narrowed my eyes at him. "There were *dozens* of people to talk to."

"Yeah, but no one interesting."

"I bet you didn't even try. I bet you just stood there and decided they weren't interesting on your own."

"Unlike you and Heather, I'm not here to try and make new friends—or get dates."

"Well, maybe that's why you're doing

everything you can to make sure *we* don't," I said.

"What? I was just making sure you were safe, that's all."

"I can take care of myself, Spencer."

"You don't know this guy very well. Should you really be up there alone with him?"

"Okay, so, what's your plan? Are you going to follow me around this entire trip? And what about when we both get to Linden, will you follow me around there, too?"

He looked absolutely appalled. "God, no."

"Because, for someone who acts like he doesn't care and claims he doesn't care—you sure seem to care."

"I don't . . . care. I just think you should be a little more choosy, that's all."

"Gee. Could you be any ruder?" I responded, then I stormed out of the room. Who was he to tell me to be more choosy? I'd chosen *him* once. Did he not see the irony there? Not that I'd do it again, because he'd obviously gotten even more conceited over the past two years.

I decided not to go back to the party—it had ended on a fairly decent note, considering, unless you counted Spencer's interruption, which I didn't. I'd ruin any magic Blake and I had if I went back now and sort of lamely stood there with a pop, waiting for something else to happen.

I changed into my pajamas and lay down on my bed, totally exhausted. I picked up my camera and started going through all the pictures I'd taken that day, deciding which ones to keep and which to delete so I could free up my memory card.

As I went through them, skipping all the ones with Spencer, I thought about how Blake had touched my hair, how he'd slipped his hands around my waist while we looked at pictures earlier, how we'd been semi-snuggled.

Blake had actually been here, in my room. Maybe that was moving things along too fast, but come on—would anything seriously happen with seven adults downstairs? I mean, I guess it could have, and maybe it would have . . . and was I actually ready for that? Me, the person who couldn't even manage one decent kiss with a guy?

What was I thinking, inviting him up here? Maybe Spencer was right.

No. Spencer can't be right. That would make him even more conceited.

Maybe he could be right without me telling him that he was. Maybe then it wouldn't count.

Chapter 8

"*D*on't forget the tomatoes!"

The next morning, I'd been dragged to the supermarket by my mom to help buy groceries. And I do mean dragged. Out of bed. Feet first.

It was our family's turn to cook dinner that night, and Mom insisted I give her some input, even though she'd already made all the decisions. She was calling the evening "Fiesta! Night" and had grand ideas about decorating, appetizers, and *flan*.

I wasn't sure what sort of input there was left for me to give her. She had the whole thing pretty much figured out, start to finish. My mom is a great hostess but she can really get carried away with her concepts. I definitely wasn't looking forward to spending half my afternoon in the kitchen with her, preparing things. (Not that burritos and tacos take that long to make—for anyone *else*, that is.)

We'd already decided to have fish tacos, chicken burritos, and cheese enchiladas. Now she was picking out the perfect limes to slice for decoration in the frozen margaritas for the adults, and then kiwis for kiwi-lime slushees for us "under twenty-ones."

Then we had to get cilantro, lettuce, tomatoes, and three different kinds of hot peppers.

Everyone else in our group, right now, was either buying a kite, or flying a kite at the beach. The entire van had headed to Kitty Hawk Kites, because it was a breezy morning and because they were all going to do something fun.

Me? I was standing in the produce section with a perfectionist.

"How about we just order in?" I suggested. "I bet there's a very good—"

"Em. Try to get into the spirit of things."

"Olé," I muttered.

She smiled briefly. "That's more like it."

We hit the dairy case and picked up sour cream, cheese, and eggs. We reviewed tortilla types, corn versus flour, large versus small. We got various types of chips. We got enough snacks and lunch things for our family of three to last us through the next millennium. Finally, the cart was full, and we were approaching the registers, looking for a line that wasn't five-deep, when I saw Blake come striding into the store.

My heart started to pound the way it used to before a ballet solo as I watched him disappear down an aisle. *Aisle 4*, I committed to memory.

"You know what, Mom? I just thought of something that we still need," I said, already starting to move away, before I lost track of which aisle Blake had entered. "Black olives."

"Oh?" My mother's face scrunched into a worried frown. "What do we need them for?" she asked as if I were suggesting we put them on breakfast cereal.

"Have you ever tasted a burrito without

them?" I asked.

"Yes, plenty of times," she said calmly.

"Oh, I know—I was thinking of the enchiladas, then. They definitely call for black olives."

"You know, you're right. But is it green or black?"

"Black." I didn't have time to stand in line debating culinary choices. "You wait here in line," I told her. "I'll be right back."

"If you're getting them, make sure you get enough!" she called after me. "There's nothing worse than running out!"

I raced around the store, trying to figure out where Blake had gone. I ran past three aisles before I spotted him just at the end of the canned veggies, fruits, and "international condiments" area, putting a jar of salsa into the basket he carried on his arm.

"Hey! What are you doing here?" I said all in a rush, so maybe he didn't even hear how stupid it sounded.

"Hey, Emily. How's it going?" he asked. He flashed a broad smile at me, and I think that I actually sighed with pleasure—but thankfully not very loudly. "What are you up to?"

"Not much. Olives," I said.

"Really. Olives." He looked at me and nodded. "You came all the way down here for olives."

"You know. A girl gets a, um, craving." I laughed, embarrassed. Why did I just say that? I considered toppling the pyramid of canned peaches behind me just to distract him from my stupid babbling. "Actually, I'm here with my mom."

God. That was even worse.

"We're supposed to cook tonight," I went on. "So anyway, I—"

Before I could get another word out, Blake leaned down and kissed me. On the lips.

Eek! What is this? I wondered as I attempted to get over the shock and kiss him back.

"You know what? You're cute when you're flustered," he said.

"I wasn't," I said feebly. "Flustered." *However, now, I definitely am,* I thought as he kissed me a second time.

I closed my eyes and wondered when my mother would run up, shrieking, "Emily! You don't kiss in grocery stores! Emergency, Aisle Four!"

"Um . . ." I said as he broke off the kiss. What was I supposed to say? Thanks, that was nice? Got any more where that came from? What gum do you chew, because that was cinnamony? I think I love you?

"Y'all should come out with us tonight," he said, backing up. "There's a great band playing in town. It's an all-ages show."

"Oh, yeah?" Was he inviting me to go out with him? Or them, anyway? "Cool."

"The guys and I are going down to Ocracoke for the day, so I've got to run. Just grabbing some food for the trip."

I glanced at the basket over his arm, which was filled with chips and candy. I didn't see any okra, not that I'd recognize it. "Okra-what?" I asked him.

"Ocracoke. The island?" He was walking backward, smiling.

"Oh, yeah. I saw that in the guidebook." I

smiled, wondering if it was too late to suggest we all go there, too. Knowing my mom, it was planned for a specific day and time, down to the minute. An impromptu sprint to the ferry—on Fiesta! Night—wouldn't cut it.

"So, see you tonight? How about if we meet y'all on the beach at eight, like, at the bottom of the steps?" Blake suggested. "If anything changes, just drop by, okay? If we're not home, leave a note on the door. Hey, have a great day!" He smiled and waved good-bye.

I felt my life changing in that exact moment, right by the cans of black olives.

When I got back to the line, in a complete and utter daze, Mom was already through and standing with the cart full of grocery bags, looking around impatiently for me. I smiled when I saw her and waved. I sort of drifted into line. I had to pay for a couple of cans of black olives, but it was well worth the two dollars.

"You're in a good mood," Mom commented as I loaded all the paper bags into the trunk of the car.

When I closed it, the Rustbucket gave up a

few pieces of rust, flaking off onto my hand. "Oh, you know. Just glad we got this done, so we can go enjoy the rest of the day," I said.

"Me too. Now I have two more errands before we head home. . . ."

I wanted to get back to the house and share the good news with Heather. "But Mom. The meat—shouldn't it go in the fridge?"

"Yes, but it should be fine for a little while."

"Really? Because it's like eighty-nine degrees out. And didn't you get some frozen stuff, too?" I couldn't believe I had to point that out to her. She was usually the queen of food safety.

"Well, true. Would you mind if maybe I stop by the house and drop off you and the groceries—then go back out on my own?"

"Sounds great," I said. "I'll get the guys to help unload stuff."

My mother snorted. "Yeah, right."

"What do you mean?"

She slid into the driver's seat. "You have a lot to learn about boys."

Well, whose fault is that, Mrs. Overprotective? I

wanted to ask, but didn't. I needed to stay on her good side—on *all* her good sides.

As she turned out of the parking lot, the car made a high, squealing sound as if we'd just run over a piglet. "What was that?" I asked.

"Don't ask," she mumbled.

I sat back and thought about Blake's kisses in the canned vegetables aisle. Who would have thought that I'd have the most romantic encounter of my life at a grocery store?

After I put all the food away, I went outside and found Heather on the beach, flying a colorful kite with Adam and the twins, Tim and Tyler. I managed to pull her away for a few minutes so we could dish in private.

"I saw Blake at the grocery store. I mean . . . I *saw* him, saw him." I quickly told her the story and how he'd mentioned going to the club together that night. "It was the weak-in-the-knees type kiss."

"Seriously?"

"Seriously. And also? Plural," I said. "Then again, I don't know. I could've been weak-kneed because I didn't have breakfast yet. But still, it was shocking. And nice."

"That's so awesome!" She squeezed my arm. "For me, last night's party was kind of a bust. Didn't you think? I kept trying to hang out with Trevor, but there were so many people. He's really popular."

"He definitely seems to be," I agreed. "What about some of the other guys?"

"I'm not sure any of them even noticed me—there were so many other girls around." She shrugged.

"Not notice *you*? Impossible."

"I'm short. And then I went outside onto the deck for some air, and I saw my mom sitting over here by herself," Heather explained. "I had to go see if she was all right. We went for a walk, got some ice cream."

"Did you guys . . . have an okay time? Good ice cream?"

She laughed. "We bond over ice cream. So, yeah. But I totally missed anything happening for me at the party. But you—wow! Last time I saw you, you took off with Blake. How did that go?"

"Fine, until Spencer butted in."

"He did what? Hold that thought." She glanced at her phone, which had started to ring. "Unknown caller. Great," she said. "Just what I need."

I shrugged. "You never know."

"Hello? Oh. Oh! Hi. This is Heather. Yeah, of course I remember you guys. God, you don't think I give out my number to *everyone*, do you?" She covered the end of the phone with her hand and whispered, "It's the guys from Currituck. Corolla. Whatever!"

"You're kidding!" I whispered.

"So you're wondering what we're doing tonight?" she said. "Well . . . I think we're going to this place. Can't remember the name of it, but there's a club and live music — Yes! That one. You can meet us? Oh, great. That sounds awesome. Okay, see you then, Dean."

She closed her phone and we both looked at it, and each other, and burst out laughing. "See, good things happen when you take a risk or two. You're with Blake, and now I might have a chance with one of them —"

"I'm not *with* Blake," I said. "I mean, not totally."

"You kissed him! I think that counts for something," Heather said. "Unless you're planning on going farther?"

"No, I'm not. Absolutely not," I said.

"Unless, of course . . . you change your mind." Heather wiggled her eyebrows. "Heat of the moment and all."

"Shut up," I said. "If that happens? I'll unheat. Okay?"

That afternoon, we quickly ran the going-out plan past Heather's mother, just to let her know. Of course, she had her own idea, which involved getting chaperones. It took us a while to convince her that Adam and Spencer would make good chaperones—then we had to actually convince Adam and Spencer.

We walked over to where they were standing in the surf, talking while they watched a big freighter out at sea. Spencer was holding a book, and Adam was dressed to go for a run.

"Will you guys go out with us tonight to a

club? My mom said you need to go with us, so we don't "look vulnerable,'" Heather said, making air quotes with her fingers. "Whatever that means."

"I'm not sure I get this. Why should we tag along just so you can go out with a random guy?" Spencer asked.

"They're not random," I said.

"They?" repeated Adam.

"We met Dean and his friend—the lighthouse guys—already, and then there's Blake. We already know him," Heather said.

"Not well," Spencer reminded me.

Actually? Better and better all the time, I thought, remembering again how Blake and I had kissed in the canned veggies section. I *hadn't* forgotten how nice it felt and I hoped he hadn't, either. But it definitely wasn't something I'd share with Spencer, who suddenly cut into my thoughts with, "You know, it never works out with the girl next-door. That's a total myth."

"Speaking from experience?" I asked.

"No, I'm just saying it's a stereotype, the whole girl-next-door, boy-next-door thing. It's like what you wish would happen, that this person you've known for a long time ends up being wonderful and you're perfectly matched, and you live happily ever after because they realize how incredibly fantastic you are, too."

"Dude. You sound jaded." Heather grinned. "I am totally going to ask your parents what this is all about. I bet your mom could tell me stories."

"There's no story, it's just an observation," Spencer said.

"Right. It just came out of *nowhere*. I'm sure," Heather teased him. "Anyway, you don't even know these guys."

"Maybe not, but neither do you," said Spencer. "I'm not trying to be mean, but if you think you're going to end up anywhere near Bl—"

"Bitter, jaded, pessimistic. What *aren't* you?" I interrupted.

"Your personal chaperone," Spencer replied calmly, giving me a look that was very close to *You're annoying me, you children. Go away.*

"Look, I already said *I'd* go," said Adam.

"What are you guys waiting for?"

"You're the best. Thanks." I hugged him, and as I did, I caught Spencer's eye. Why was he looking at me like that? Like everything I did bothered him? "Do you have a problem?" I asked.

"What kind of problem?" he replied.

"I don't know," I said. "With me? With us going out to this club tonight?"

"Going out?"

"Are you just going to repeat everything I say?" I asked.

"Am I repeating everything you say? I didn't realize," he said.

I sighed in exasperation as Heather, Adam, and Spencer all laughed at me. I grabbed Spencer's book out of his hands and tossed it into the ocean.

"Hey! Hey! You don't drown Homer!" he yelled, diving in after the book.

Chapter 9

"*Y*'all dance really well," Blake said.

Did he mean me? I wondered. Or did he mean everyone? This "y'all" thing was confusing.

"Oh, well . . . thanks." I could tell him how many years of lessons I'd taken, how I'd studied ballet but also modern, interpretive, hip-hop, and jazz dance. But the place was so loud, it was impossible to hear or say much. Besides, I couldn't help thinking that anything I said might sound like I was bragging, and that would definitely be an annoying quality. "Thanks," I repeated.

"Thanks for what?" he asked, having already forgotten the subject.

"Oh, um. The dance. The club. You know, what's funny is that, like, if everyone had access to a place like this, then people would probably dance better." I wished I hadn't said that. I was starting to sound like Miss Teen South Carolina.

"What?" Blake asked.

I heaved a sigh of relief that he hadn't heard me. "Nothing," I said. "Not important."

We'd gotten to the club around nine o'clock. We'd all walked there together, traveling in a pack. Me, Blake, Heather, Trevor, and Adam. Spencer refused to show up before ten, because he said it wasn't cool. As if he'd know.

The minute we walked through the door and got our hands stamped, Adam bumped into a guy he knew from going to a baseball training camp during spring break in Florida. They started talking baseball, and the rest of us moved on to hanging out by the dance floor, then actually dancing to a couple of songs.

When the band went on break, Blake and Trevor took off with a mission to talk to the band about doing a show near their college in the fall.

Before Heather and I could even talk about how things were going, she grabbed my arm.

"Hey, look who's here!" she cried.

I scanned the club, expecting to see a celebrity from the tone of her voice. "Who?"

"Dean and Chase," she said. "The lighthouse boys."

"Formerly known as orange shirt and blue shirt." I checked them out as they stood at the top of the steps, near the entrance. "They're taller than I remembered. And cuter!" I said.

"No doubt," Heather agreed. "I wish I knew which one was which, but oh well, I'll find out. It's not like they know our names, either. I've got to run. See you—"

"What? You can't leave me!" I protested. "They live here, which means they probably know tons of people—"

"Maybe, but I invited them to meet *me*. I can't let them stand over there looking clueless by themselves," Heather said. "That wouldn't be nice."

"They don't look clueless," I said. "*I* look clueless."

Heather swatted my shoulder. "You do not. Just get to know Blake. Get him to talk about himself. That's all you have to do." She squeezed my arm before she walked off. "Wish me luck!"

"Wish *you* luck? What about me?" I called after her, but the music drowned out my voice. "Come back! Heather. Heath—Heather—" I was panting when Blake returned from talking to the band.

"Everything okay?" Blake asked.

"Sure . . . everything's . . . cool," I said, as slowly as possible, stalling for time, wishing I knew how I was supposed to go about this. I didn't know how to pick up a guy and just have a fling. I wasn't cut out for this stuff. What made me think that just because I was in another state, I could do it now?

We might have kissed, but we had nothing to talk about.

"You, um, come to this place . . . like, pretty often?" I said.

"Now and then." Blake shrugged.

We stood side by side, just sort of nodding to each other and looking around the crowd. I was watching Heather laugh and enjoy herself with Dean and Chase. I didn't see Adam anywhere. He'd probably left to play baseball outside or something, I decided. So much for sticking around and protecting me and Heather. I couldn't imagine he really wanted that job in the first place. Spencer sure didn't—he wasn't even here yet.

"Where's, uh, Trevor?" I asked.

"Ran into someone he knows," Blake said. "Heather?"

"Same. Pretty much. I mean, she doesn't know them well, but . . ." I found myself at a complete loss for words. I was just standing there, twirling my hair, like a complete ditz. It was like I needed a time-out to collect myself. That, or I needed to run out of the place without looking back. "You know what? I'm really thirsty—you want a pop?"

Blake looked confused. "A pop?"

"Something to drink. With fizz? That's what we call soda in the Midwest," I explained.

"Oh, a Coke. That's what we call it here," Blake said.

"Really? Right, a Coke. I've heard that. So, would you like a Coke? Or a Pepsi? Or a root beer?" I asked.

He shook his head. "Nah, I'm fine, thanks."

"Mountain Dew?" I offered.

He laughed. "No, it's just called Coke."

"What is?"

"Never mind."

"Right."

It took me forever just to get across the club, and then there was a long line at the bar, probably because the band was on break. I tried to edge closer and was making progress, until I felt a tap on my shoulder. I turned around, ready to apologize for stepping on someone's toe.

"Fancy seeing you here," Spencer said.

"Fancy? Okay, Grandpa," I replied, staring at his outfit of blue plaid madras shorts and a striped green shirt. It was almost cool. *Almost.* "What are you doing here? I thought you were staying home and reading the *Iliad* or something."

"It's the *Odyssey*. Which is kind of the way

I'd describe waiting for this bartender to notice us."

"I know. I just want a pop—a Coke," I corrected myself.

"Poppa Coke? Who's that?" he joked.

I glared at him, then sidled up to the bar a little more, pushing my way between two girls who were both on their phones and didn't even notice me. Spencer made his way past some guys walking away, beers in hand, and the two of us were suddenly only a body or two away from the actual bar. Finally, I got a chance to order.

When we both had our drinks, we pushed our way back out of the crowd. I was actually hoping to lose Spencer in the crowd, but no such luck—he stepped in front of me as I tried to get past him. "Where's your partner in crime?" Spencer asked.

"Which one?"

"Heather."

"Oh, she's over there." I gestured vaguely in case Spencer was thinking of heading over and embarrassing her.

"What happened to Adam? Wasn't he supposed to be watching you?"

"Watching us? No. Hanging around at the same place as us in case we need him? Yeah, I guess. Something like that. Anyway, he's here somewhere. He ran into some guy he met at a baseball camp this spring. It's all baseball, all the time." I took a sip of my cold pop. "What's a ribbie?"

"RBI," Spencer said. "Stands for Runs Batted In. Like, if you're at bat and you get a hit and the runner on third scores. You get credited with a ribbie."

It was like listening to someone speak Russian. It sounded nice, mysterious, and completely foreign. Maybe I had been living in a ballet bubble for too long.

"You know, if you want to talk to random guys you're going to have to brush up on your sports," Spencer commented.

"I don't want to talk to random guys," I said.

"Don't you? Seems like that's all you and Heather have been trying to do," he said.

"Oh. Well, *here*, maybe. At home, not so much."

"Really," Spencer said.

"Really. At home I just try to talk to guys I already know." I paused, taking another sip of my pop. "That doesn't go so well, either."

Spencer looked at me, and we just started laughing. I was giggling, even. It was like I'd just confessed to a crime. We were laughing the way we did when we were little kids.

Then I straightened up and headed back over to Blake, who was sitting with Trevor at a small table, a level up from the main floor.

Blake smiled up at me and I sat down in the one empty chair. "So. How often do you guys come here?" I asked.

"Here? This place?"

"Well, sure, here, or the Outer Banks, or Kill Devil Hills . . ."

"Hey, isn't that guy staying with you?" Trevor pointed to Spencer, who was standing around vaguely near us, without coming over. "Tell him to come sit with us."

"No, that's okay," I said. "I mean, he's fine.

He wants to be by himself."

"He does?" asked Blake, looking confused.

"He's strange. He, uh, reads a lot," I said, as if that were a crime. "Kind of an outsider, loner-type deal."

"Really? I talked to him a couple of times. Thought he was really cool," said Trevor. "Yo!" he called, waving to Spencer. "What's his name again?" he asked me.

"Spencer," I said with a sigh.

"Yo, Spencer!" Trevor called.

"Hey, what's up?" Spencer came over and gave the two guys brief, cool handshakes, the kind guys do that work, unlike their pretend-hugs.

"Pull up a chair," Blake offered.

"No, it's all right, he was just leaving. Weren't you?" I said.

"Thanks." Spencer ignored me and pulled a chair over from a nearby table. "So. You guys both go to UNC, right? I think Emily said that."

Blake nodded. "Yeah, it's our last year. Well, unless I screw up."

"Why would you do that?" I asked.

"Who wants to graduate? Then you have to get a job and work the rest of your life," Blake explained.

"Good point."

"What about you guys?" said Trevor.

"We're only going to be freshmen next year," Spencer said. "Technically, I could be a sophomore, so I'm calling it my freshomore year."

Could you be any freshomore annoying? I wanted to say.

"Where are you going?" Blake asked.

"Linden College," I said.

"Never heard of it."

"No, you wouldn't—I mean, it's a small college in Michigan."

"I thought y'all were from Wisconsin." Blake looked confused. "You know, cheese-heads."

"And how do you guys know each other again?" Trevor asked.

"Our dads have been friends since college, so . . ."

"They set you up!" Trevor nodded. "I get it."

"No!" I coughed. "No, we just have these group reunions. In groups. It's a very big *group*."

"Emily's the youngest in the *group*," Spencer said, seemingly out of nowhere.

"I am not," I said. "The twins are only four. They're practically infants. So no, I'm not the youngest."

Trevor, Blake, and Spencer started laughing at how defensive I was being. "Well, as long as you're older than *four*," Spencer said. "Then I guess it's okay for you to be here."

I scooted over a little closer to Blake. Then I leaned over and suggested quietly, "Maybe we should go outside."

"Outside? Why would we go outside?"

"So we could have some privacy. You know." I gestured toward Spencer and Trevor. "Like last night. On the balcony?"

"Yeah. Well, I can't go anywhere. I'm supposed to be meeting someone."

"Meeting someone? Like, other friends?"

Suddenly, a tall girl with spiky red hair, wearing a short black dress and tall black boots, came up to our table and dropped herself into Blake's lap.

"Where have you been? Oh, my God, I thought I wasn't going to see you again!" She planted a big kiss on his lips. "I missed you so much!"

Blake grinned and kissed her back, nuzzling her neck. "I told you I'd be here tonight, didn't I? Where have you been? I thought y'all were going to be here at nine."

Y'all. Why had I ever thought that was a cute expression? It was annoying, especially when it meant "not you, Emily—*her.*"

Chapter 10

"*Y*ou know, I was doing fine until *you* came along," I muttered to Spencer as the band took the stage again. Blake and Mystery Girl had run off to the dance floor together, while I'd moved to a darker, less conspicuous area, so I could feel like an idiot in private. Spencer had followed me, no doubt so I could hear him gloat over the loud music.

"I think you mean until she came along," Spencer said. "Because I'm not the one who jumped into his lap."

I sighed and leaned against the railing. I thought that when Blake and I had kissed it actually meant something. Not a lot, maybe, but something. Apparently, I was just one of the many girls around here he kissed. But I didn't want to talk about it with Spencer.

"Why don't you make yourself useful and go check on Heather or something?" I asked.

He pointed to Heather, who was dancing with one of the guys from Corolla. "She seems to be doing fine."

"What are you talking about? She's all over him! They're so close they could be arrested in some states," I said. "Go break them up, why don't you?"

"Relax. They're just dancing."

"You know, I think I know why you agreed to come tonight."

"I can't resist the pull of a bad cover band?"

I narrowed my eyes and glared at him. "You can't stand the idea of me, of us, having fun without you. Having fun, period. Being happy. You probably knew about Blake and what's-her-name."

"Look, I didn't want to upset you, but . . . I never thought you and Blake were on the same page."

"What are you talking about? We just met,

we still have to get to know each other, and—anyway, I'm sure she's just an old friend, and there's nothing wrong with friends."

"No, unless you have, like, seven of them. And you kiss all of them."

"What are you saying?"

"Emily, come on. Look. Didn't you see him and that girl?"

"But he's nice. He loaned me his sweat-shirt."

"A sweatshirt isn't a relationship."

I frowned at him. "Are you thinking of putting that saying on a T-shirt? Because don't."

"I'm sorry, Emily, but the guy seems kind of like a player. Come on, I'll walk you home," Spencer said.

"Why would I leave just because Blake is dancing with someone . . . else?" I yanked my arm away from his. The last thing I wanted was his pity. "Just leave me alone, okay?" I narrowed my eyes at him. "What are you wearing, anyway? Plaid and stripes should only be worn by rock stars, like Gwen Stefani, or someone on *Project Runway*."

"I think I'm crushed. Hold on," he said. He waited a few seconds and checked his pulse. "Nope. Still fine."

"Well, as much as this night is starting to suck, we're still not leaving. We can't just go and leave Heather here on her own."

"I'll tell Adam we're going. He can be in charge of her."

I laughed. "Do you think anyone can be in charge of Heather? Do you know Heather at all? Besides, has anyone seen Adam? I bet he's off playing baseball somewhere, some all-night lighted playing . . . place."

"Field. Or diamond. Baseball diamond," Spencer said.

"Whatever."

"Your dad's really into sports. How do you not know all these basic things that any six-year-old would know?" Spencer asked, making me sound like the dumbest person on the planet, or at least in the room.

"And how do you not have better manners than a six-year-old? How do you go around just insulting people without even noticing?"

"What? I do not."

"You constantly do," I argued.

"Look. If this is about what happened, you know, in the Dells—"

"It isn't."

That was the second time he'd brought it up, but we hadn't actually talked about it. I definitely wasn't in the mood to now. A person can only take so much rejection in one night.

We sat silently, watching people dance. I sipped my ice, then tipped the cup back and chewed some ice. All I wanted was to get out of there, but at the same time, I wanted to hang around and see how Heather was doing, make sure she was all right—make sure *she* had a better night than I did.

Spencer was apparently watching her, too. "Hey, is that orange shirt or blue shirt with Heather?" he asked. "I thought you had dibs on blue shirt."

I laughed, despite the fact I sort of wanted to slug him. "Shut up. I don't have dibs on anyone," I said. "Isn't it obvious?"

"Hey. If we need to kill time, I could always

tell you the girl-next-door story," Spencer offered.

"For real?"

"Sure."

"Should I get a tissue?" I asked.

"For me, yeah. A box." He cleared his throat. "Don't get your hopes up—it's not a very long or interesting—"

"Just tell it," I urged. I was dying for something else to think about.

"Okay. Like I said, it's not a very long story. There was this girl, next door. Well, three doors down. Her name was Morgan. Still is, actually. I wanted to ask her to prom," Spencer began. "But we were kind of friends, you know, so it had to be really creative, had to blow her away. I kept plotting how to do it. I had a hundred brilliant ideas. Romantic ones. Thoughtful ones. Funny ones. In the end? Someone else asked her before I even tried *one* of my ideas."

I started laughing. Harder and harder.

"You think that's funny?"

"No. No! Yes! See, that kind of sort of happened to me, too."

"Well, I'm glad I could *amuse* you. Now, don't go anywhere. I'll be right back," Spencer said.

I surveyed the dance floor, checking on Heather.

Did Blake have to dance right there? In plain sight? Why didn't he go somewhere private—say, back to Georgia?

And what was he thinking, anyway? That it was okay to have two girls interested in him at the same time? Maybe I should go over there right now and make out with him, the way she jumped on his lap when I was talking to him. It wasn't too late. I could fight for him.

Did I want to, though? Did it matter?

"Hey. Spencer got me. Dragged me away, actually," Heather said, glaring over at him.

"He's good at that."

"I told him to wait for us over there so we could talk." She gave me a little hug. "He told me what happened. Don't take this thing with Blake personally. He's an idiot, that's all. Anyway, you more than accomplished your goal. You had a summer fling!"

"That counts? We only kissed twice. At a Publix."

"It counts."

"Right. Then why do I feel so bad that it's over all of a sudden?"

"Flings are like that. You can't take them too seriously."

That was easy for her to say. It meant a lot to me when I kissed someone—or it was supposed to.

"You know what? Maybe that wasn't the perfect fling. Maybe you need to set your sights on someone else."

"No thanks."

"Yes," Heather insisted. "Because Dean and I—we're totally hitting it off. He's very cool. And you know what? Maybe you could go out with his friend, Chase. I'll set something up!" she said excitedly.

I shook my head. "No, don't bother—it's okay."

"Emily, this vacation is far from over. Do you want to mope around or do you want to show Blake you can find someone else, too?"

I didn't really care about showing up Blake—I probably wouldn't ever see him again. "Can't I just sit here feeling crushed for a little while?"

"Fine, but I think you're overreacting," Heather said.

"I'm not," I said. "I was really into him! And he invited us here, and now he's making out with another girl!"

Heather gave one last look across the club. "Hmm. I see your point. You want to get out of here?"

"Thought you'd never ask," I sighed.

"Only . . . do you think you can wait a second while I go tell Dean good-bye?" she asked.

"Of course! Take your time," I told her. *Only . . . not too much, because I really want to bolt and every second of this is killing me*, I thought as I smiled at her, trying to put my best face on a bad situation.

"Emily, get whatever you want," Heather said when she slid into a booth at an all-night breakfast place fifteen minutes later. "We're treating."

"We are?" Spencer asked.

"Duh. It's tradition," Heather said. "The person who has the worst night gets treated to breakfast afterward."

"That's not fair. You haven't asked about *my* night," Adam said, pouting.

"Or mine, either," Spencer added, taking a sip of ice water.

"Fine." Heather set down her menu and faced them. "Do tell."

"Yeah. And don't leave anything out, we want all the details," I said, leaning against the wall.

Adam glanced at Spencer. "You want to go first?"

"Sure. Well, I went to this club. The band was supposed to be great, but it was mostly bad cover songs. I ran into some friends. And there was this one girl who would *not* leave me alone."

"You don't mean *me*," I said.

"If the shoe fits . . ." Spencer said.

"Shut up! You should be so lucky. You're the one who wouldn't leave my side."

"As if," Spencer replied. "I tried to leave about a hundred times. You just wanted to stay, for some unknown reason." He turned to Adam. "What happened to you, anyway? I didn't see you all night."

"First I ran into this guy from baseball camp. Then we went to hang out with some guys he knew. We went for pizza, then we hit an arcade, then we ran into more people—"

"Was it fun?" Heather asked.

"Sure. I just felt bad because I ditched you guys," Adam said.

"We've been ditched much worse than that tonight," I muttered. "Don't worry about it."

"Why? What happened?" Adam looked confused.

"Never mind," I said. "Let's talk about something else."

"Okay. Do you guys want to hear about Dean?" Heather asked.

"You know, I'm not sure if I should get the

pancakes or the waffles. Can we have a table vote?" asked Spencer, trying to change the subject.

When we got our food, I wasn't all that hungry, so I started taking pictures instead. I got Spencer checking his reflection in the stainless-steel napkin dispenser, Heather trying to keep her long hair out of the maple syrup, and Adam's hands shaking as he had his fourth cup of coffee.

For a while I was having so much fun that I almost completely forgot that I'd been blown off in a major way by the first guy I'd really, actually ever kissed.

Chapter 11

"So, are you guys ready for today's tour?" my mother asked, in an upbeat, chipper mood that couldn't have been more opposite of mine.

We were gathered out back of the house, by the minivan. I'd managed to haul myself out of bed and swallow a couple of sips of coffee before I'd been rounded up for the trip. Everyone was going, which meant I had to, even though I felt more like spending the day in bed, recovering. Not from partying, mind you—from *lack* of partying. From extreme heartbreak, or at least, disappointment.

"Have a bagel, honey," Heather's mother said, holding a paper plate out to me. "You'll feel better."

"Thanks." I took a half and nibbled a corner of it. *But I doubt it.* I leaned against the van and closed my eyes, wishing I were back in bed. I heard the sound of flip-flops snapping toward me and finally opened my eyes, expecting to see Adam or Heather.

"Good morning, y'all!" Blake had sauntered over to greet us. "Where you off to?"

Ugh. I nearly choked on the tiny bite of bagel I'd just swallowed.

He was the last person I wanted to see. And what was with his attitude? Was he so clueless that he didn't realize what had happened the night before—that he'd been a total jerk? His long, green preppy Bermuda shorts and polo shirt didn't seem so cute anymore. Neither did his tattooed ankle, his spiky platinum hair, his cut body, and his habit of saying "y'all."

"We're going on a drive. See some things," I said. "Lots of things. Cape Hatteras, you know."

"That'll be fun," said Blake. "If only you could ditch the parents . . ." he said out of the corner of his mouth.

"Oh, they're not so bad," I said.

Heather came racing around the corner of the house as if someone had just summoned her. Spencer was right behind her, walking at a fast clip.

"Morning, y'all," Blake greeted them.

"Oh, hi," Spencer said casually. "Didn't see you."

"Wow. Are people still wearing those?" Heather asked, pointing at the obnoxious Bermuda shorts.

"I know my great-grandfather has some," Spencer said. "Drags 'em out every summer for the family reunion."

It wasn't much of a put-down, but I smiled just the same. Blake was glancing down at his outfit, confused. He brushed at some sand sticking on his ankle, by his tattoo.

"Hey, Blake, I've been meaning to ask— what's that tattoo of?"

"It's a chili pepper," Blake said. "Got it in Mexico."

"Really? Is it one of those stick-on ones? Because it looks like it's coming off," said Adam as he approached us from the backyard.

"So what's that supposed to mean? You're hot?" asked Heather.

"Looks like a banana," Spencer observed. "Maybe it's supposed to mean he's bananas?"

"Yeah. Well, it's a jalapeño," Blake said, sounding a little stung that we weren't impressed. "Anyway, I have to go."

"Us too. Have a great day. Y'all," I tacked on bitterly as Heather nearly dragged me into the minivan.

"Good riddance, y'all!" she added with a giggle.

"In the van again . . . I just can't wait to be in the van again."

I groaned at my father's reworking of "On the Road Again." He was almost ruining the beautiful scenery we were passing through on the long, narrow coastal road. There were sand dunes on both sides of us, and sand drifted across the road in places. "Dad, please," I begged.

He kept singing, though. His voice carried. And carried. And carried.

"Dad!" I urged again.

"What?"

"You sang that yesterday," I said. "And the day before. You are embarrassing the entire van."

"Someone's in a good mood," Adam commented.

"Do vans get embarrassed?" Spencer asked. "I'm not sure, I've never seen a van blush—"

"Shut up," I said over my shoulder.

"Emily!" my mother said. "That's not very nice."

"Sorry," I mumbled.

"Like I said: Mood. Not good. Don't provoke her," Adam told Spencer.

"Right. That intense inner ballerina comes out, and when she does, take cover," Spencer teased. "She'll go ballistic in a *Swan Lake* kind of way."

Despite the fact he'd sort of come to my rescue the night before, I wasn't in the mood to be mocked by Spencer. Not that I ever was, but that day in particular, I felt very thin-skinned.

But *not* in a ballet dancer way, whatever that was. They should check out a ballet dancer's feet sometime and see just how thick the skin could get when you danced on it every day for hours. Mine had gotten a little softer over the past year, but not much.

Anyway, I felt thin-skinned over the whole Blake episode. Everyone knew that I'd liked him; now they knew he was not into me. I was desperately hoping that we could put it behind us. Getting away from the house for the day was a great idea, even if it meant listening to my dad sing.

In the grand scheme of things, Blake didn't mean all that much to me. I'd remember his shoulders. The way he could wear board shorts and his rock-hard abs. I'd show his picture to my friends at home and tell them how he'd invited me to a party, how he'd loaned me his sweatshirt, how I'd kissed him a few times. That was all true.

It would sound good, in retrospect. Running into him over the rest of our stay would be awkward and embarrassing, but I could handle it.

We pulled into the parking lot of Bodie Island Lighthouse, and Spencer sighed. "Here we go again. Seen one lighthouse, you've seen 'em all," he complained.

"Not really," I said, scooting over to the door to get out of the van. "This one's got stripes."

"As opposed to what?" He climbed out of the backseat. "Polka dots?"

"Just be a good tourist for once in your life, okay?" I sort of snapped at him.

"Maybe you could stop by the gift shop for some chocolate," he suggested before walking away with Adam. "Like, a pound."

While Heather veered off from the group to use her cell phone, my mother slipped into place beside me. "What's wrong?" she asked.

I shook my head. "Nothing."

"Your shoulders always slump when something's wrong. Your posture goes south. So tell me, what is it?"

I tried to raise my shoulders back to their regular height, because I didn't want to talk about it with her, at least not right now.

"Did something happen last night?" Mom asked.

"It just wasn't that much fun," I said. "Loud music, rude people. You know how it is."

"Oh. Well, better luck next time, hon," she said, then she hurried to catch up with Heather's mom.

What, did she have something better to do?

I didn't know whether to feel insulted or elated as I meandered along around the light-house park grounds. I mean, it was great that Mom had friends and that the spotlight wasn't on me, for a change. But I could have at least used a hug.

By the time I reached the lighthouse, every-one was turning back.

"We can't tour this one," Mrs. Flanagan told me.

"What a shame," Spencer muttered.

"Look at it this way, kid." His dad slapped him on the back. "That's two hundred and four-teen steps you don't have to climb."

Spencer looked over at him. "Who said I

was going to climb?"

"Aren't you working on being a good tourist today? That's what Emily said," his father replied. "Good tourist means participating—"

Spencer lifted his father's hand off his shoulder. "Dad, I'm not eight, okay?"

"Emily. We're waiting for you!" my mother called.

"I'm here. Present and accounted for." I looked at her, not getting it. "What?"

"Before we go, don't you want to get our picture? That's your job," she said.

"Oh. Right. I forgot." I took out my camera while everyone arranged themselves in front of the visitor center sign. Other tourists were streaming in and out of the frame, but I decided it didn't matter—maybe I'd catch something unusual.

"Ready? Everyone say squeeze!" Heather yelled.

"What? Why?" commented Mrs. Flanagan. "Who am I supposed to squeeze, anyway?"

"It's an expression, Mom," Spencer said. "Roll with it."

He looked at me and rolled his eyes, like we'd both had more than enough of our parents for the morning already. I managed a small smile. "Everybody. One-two-three, squeeze!" I called, snapping a picture just as a tall man walked right in front of me.

"Oh, no. Sorry, miss. Sorry," he said.

"It's okay," I told him. "Don't worry about it."

"Let's just go down to Cape Hatteras and have our picnic lunch," my mother declared, and we headed back to the van.

"How much farther is it?" I asked.

"Oh, only about an hour and a half." She opened her backpack and pulled out a box of salt water taffy, which she handed to me. "Pass these around. It'll make the drive go faster."

"I'll sit next to you," Adam volunteered. "Just in case you need help opening the box."

"No way are you hogging the salt water taffy," Spencer said, jostling for position beside me as we climbed into the van. "Remember what happened on that trip in Maine? You ate the whole box, then got sick on the Ferris wheel."

"I was eight," said Adam.

"Those who don't learn from history are condemned to repeat it," Spencer said, settling onto the bench seat beside me.

I handed him the box. "Help yourself. Go wild."

"Why are we the only ones doing this?" Spencer asked halfway up the steps to the top of the Cape Hatteras Lighthouse.

"Adam's up there. Somewhere," I said. "So, we're not the only ones. We're the slow ones."

Heather had stayed behind and had been sipping an iced tea when we decided to take the tour. I was so jealous of her right then that I could spit. Or sweat, anyway. The back of my shirt was getting damp.

"I was only trying to be a good tourist. It's your fault. You're the one who coined the phrase and now my dad is addicted to it," Spencer said. "I didn't read the sign. How many steps is this?"

"Two hundred and sixty-eight," I said, out of breath. "The sign said that it's equivalent to climbing a twelve-story building. I thought, how hard could that be?"

Spencer coughed. "Obviously you've never lived in a twelve-story building. It's really hot in here."

"Not to mention humid," I added.

"Hey, slow down. You're going faster than I am. Maybe I shouldn't have had those twenty-five pieces of salt water taffy in the van."

"Or that country farmer's breakfast last night," I added. "Was that eight pieces of bacon or ten?"

"I don't know why we have to see the view. I mean, if you've seen one . . . lighthouse . . ." Spencer panted. "You've seen 'em . . ." Suddenly, he tripped, his foot hitting a step. He fell forward onto me and we both toppled awkwardly onto the stairs with a yelp.

"Oh, God. I'm sorry. I'm really sorry." Spencer stood up and brushed himself off.

"Maybe if you weren't barefoot—"

"I'm not barefoot!" Spencer protested.

"Then it's the fact you're not used to wearing shoes," I said as I got up and brushed some dirt off my arm. "You don't know how to walk in them."

"I tripped! I'm not a *cave*man," Spencer said.

We both walked a few steps farther, then stopped on a landing to rest. A white-haired elderly couple passed us.

"So that's who was breathing down my neck," Spencer whispered.

"They've got to be, like, sixty," I said. "This is getting embarrassing."

"Getting?"

"Hey guys, how's it going?" Adam asked, already on his way back down.

"Just great! Show-off," Spencer muttered under his breath.

"We paid seven dollars to abuse ourselves like this?" I asked. "Okay, so technically my dad paid, but . . ." No wonder Heather had stayed behind.

"I thought I was in shape," Spencer said. "I am so . . . not . . ."

"Sure you are. You're just not in as good shape as half the senior citizens here."

We both collapsed in out-of-breath, winded giggles.

"Come on, if we don't get going we'll get lapped by the next tour," I said, urging him to continue. "You go first this time."

"Fine, but Emily? And I mean this. No pictures," Spencer said. "Okay?"

"What are you thinking? That I wanted a picture of your butt?"

"Who doesn't?" he replied, posing with a little bump to the right.

Another pair of grandparents passed us on the way down and gave us a look that could have stopped—or at least slowed—stairs traffic.

"Do we have to walk all the way back down or can we just rappel?" Spencer asked.

We were standing at the edge of the top of the lighthouse, looking down at the ocean. We'd finally made it after all. "What do you think this is, *The Amazing Race*? I mean, if you want to try skydiving, go ahead, but I don't see anyone holding a mattress down there, and I don't think the ground is very soft."

"I've been skydiving before," Spencer said. "And rock climbing. The only thing I'm not so good at is walking down all those circular steps. It makes me dizzy."

"We don't have to rush back down," I said.

"Technically, we do. There's a time limit, because there's a limit to how many people can be up here at one time."

"So we'll recuperate really quickly."

"Okay, but I want to be a good tourist. Not a bad one who lurks on the side and messes things up for everyone else." He glared at me.

"Keep working at it, you have a ways to go," I said. "How about enjoying the view?" I walked around the top of the lighthouse gazing at the expanses of water and land below.

"Come on, you two—time to get going," our tour guide said. "Time to begin our descent."

"Okay, but first—can I please take a few photos?" I said.

"Sure, but make it quick." She nodded at me.

"Do you have a timer on that thing?" Spencer asked.

"Of course, but—why? We don't need a

picture of us together," I said as I focused the camera on the light at the top.

"Sure we do," Spencer said. "We're the only ones who had the legs to climb this thing."

"And Adam," I reminded him.

"Oh. Right, I forgot."

"Did you want me to get your picture planting the flag or something? You know, like people do when they climb Everest?" I teased.

"Excuse me. Sir?" Spencer approached a man standing next to us. "Would you mind taking our picture?"

"Not at all." He took the camera from me, and I showed him which button to push and explained how he had to wait to hear the little click. "Okay, guys. Stand over there. Closer, closer . . ." he urged.

"Aw. You guys make a cute couple," his wife said as we posed with big smiles, standing about a foot apart, our hands awkwardly perched on each other's shoulders, as if we were teammates on a very unclose team.

"Oh, we're not," I said.

"Of course you're cute, in fact you're

adorable—and how old are you? Sixteen, seventeen?" she went on.

Spencer frowned at her. "Nineteen. And we're not a couple," he quickly said.

"Got it!" the man said. He handed the camera to me. "I took five or six. You can delete the ones you don't want."

"Believe me, she will. She loves to delete. She *lives* to delete."

What's he talking about? I wondered, but I ignored his comment, thanked the couple, and headed for the stairs, Spencer following me. We nearly sprinted back down the spiral steps with our group. It wasn't half as much fun as the way up.

"So. We can check that off the must-see list," Spencer said as we exited. "It was definitely worth it."

"Yeah. My mom will be thrilled," I told him. "Let's eat!"

Heather jumped up as we walked over to her and said, "I finally got in touch with Dean, and it's all set."

"What's all set?" I asked.

"You meeting Chase, what else? Tonight."

"Ooh! The excitement!" Spencer said in a high-pitched voice as he waved his hands in the air.

Why was it that whenever I started to not detest him, he did something like this?

"Did I *say* that?" I asked. "Do I ever act like that?"

"Hmm. Let me think."

"You know what? Never mind. I don't *care* what you think. You're always going around telling us how you're older and how you know more and how we're so immature. Well, guess what? You're the one who's immature. And as far as going to college? I don't think you're ready, even if you are a—a so-called sopho-man."

"It's freshomore," he said in a quiet tone.

"It's annoying, is what it is." Heather headed for the van and I followed her, glad to have backup.

Chapter 12

"*How's* it going?" the young guy standing at the photo printer beside mine asked.

"Oh! Hi. Fine," I said. I'd been sitting here for an hour, editing pictures, and organizing shots, before I went ahead and made prints of the ones I wanted. "How are you?" I asked.

"Good. Tired but good."

"Yeah." I'd walked to a pharmacy to use their photo printer the next morning. I knew that according to Heather, I should be making every attempt to hit it off with this guy, that I should see what we had in common, which was easy because obviously we were both the kind of people who get up early in order to take pictures, or at least to get those pictures printed.

I could ask him about his camera. We could talk about focus and zoom features and lenses, and the rule of thirds.

But I was starting to feel like there was no point in me trying, that I was slightly-to-very jinxed when it came to guys. If I talked to this one, I'd probably end up wiping out all of his digital images or shredding all my prints by mistake. Best to just focus on the task at hand.

After I'd finished making prints, I was walking up to the counter to pay for an orange juice when I saw Spencer looking at his reflection in a twirling sunglasses display. I stopped and stared at him. "What are you doing here? You weren't following me again, were you?"

"Are you serious? Get over yourself," he replied.

His dad's head popped up from the other side of the display. He had on large, white square sunglasses that seemed more intended for Nicole Richie than him. "We're heading out in the kayak this morning. Got to have sunglasses for that. Bright sun out there on the water."

"Right. You sure do," I agreed.

"I need new sunglasses because mine fell off somewhere yesterday between the 175th and 176th steps," Spencer said.

"Really?" I checked out his reflection as he slid a pair of wire-rim glasses over his nose. "Those are very *Napoleon Dynamite.*"

He grinned and took a bow. "Thank you."

"I'm not sure it was a compliment."

He quickly pulled them off and tried on another pair. "What about these? Hmm. Well, what are you doing here?" he asked. "Did you need sunscreen or something?"

"It's personal," I said.

His face started to blush slightly. "Sorry . . . I . . ."

"It's this." I held up the brightly colored envelope with the giant word PHOTOS on the side.

Spencer looked up slowly, as if he was afraid of what he might see. "Oh! Pictures. Can I see?" he asked.

"Not yet. I mean, I'm putting them together for everyone. I want it to be a surprise."

"You are? You never said anything about that."

"You never asked. And it's a surprise, remember? So don't tell anyone," I said.

"Okay. I'll just say I saw you here . . . buying juice. They'll believe it," he said.

"I have such deep, dark secrets," I muttered.

"You want a ride back?" he asked, following me to the door.

"No, thanks. I'll walk. But maybe you should pay for those before you set off the security alarm?" I pointed to his glasses, then swept out the door.

When I got back to the house, I saw Heather lying on the beach. I quickly ran up to my room and stashed all the prints in my room's desk, changed into my bikini, then hurried outside with my hat and towel.

"Where *were* you last night?" I asked in a whisper as I dropped down to sit beside her.

"Nowhere. What do you mean?" Heather laughed. "With Dean, where else?"

"Yeah? So *tell*."

"Tell what?"

"What did you do?"

"We played mini golf. It was really cool." She smiled.

I laughed. "It was?"

"Yes. Why is that so funny?"

"I just never thought of putt-putt being . . . romantic," I said.

"Well, as a matter of fact . . . at night, with all the lights? It's actually almost cool. We had a nice time by the twirling windmill."

"Really?"

"Really. We were kissing and this older couple with their little kids was like, 'Ahem. Ahem!' They were coughing so loudly but we just pretended we didn't hear them."

"That sounds fun. So you guys are kind of an item," I said.

"We'll see. It might be a one-date thing, you never know. But I'm sorry it didn't work out to meet Chase last night."

"That's okay. I tried that whole vacation romance concept once. It didn't work out so well for me. Ahem. Exhibit A. Or should I say B."

She followed my gaze over to our next-door neighbors' deck, where Blake was standing, checking out the beach. He caught us looking his way and waved hello. I waved back, feeling kind of pathetic. "Cheers," I muttered.

I looked down at the water, where Spencer and his dad were either getting ready to go out in the double kayak, or maybe just coming back in. "Excuse me for a sec, Heather," I said, and got up and walked down to the water's edge.

"Emily! You want to try it?" Mr. Flanagan offered. "It's great fun. I'm sure Spencer would be glad to take you out."

I had this image in my head of being stranded with Spencer out on open water. He'd probably mock the way I paddled. "I don't know, I mean, you guys are all set up—"

"That's all right, I want to go get some breakfast," Mr. Flanagan said. "You ought to give it a try."

"Oh, no, Emily doesn't do any water

sports." Spencer shook his head. "She hates sports. She hates water."

I laughed. "I do not! That's not true."

I looked up and saw Blake coming closer, beach volleyball gear in hand. His red-haired girlfriend was right behind him, wearing what looked like a black vinyl—or possibly leather—swimsuit. If I had to stick around and watch the two of them, I'd go insane, or at least, more insane.

"Sure, I'd love to go kayaking," I said. "Thanks, Mr. Flanagan."

Spencer nearly dropped the kayak paddle. "Really?"

"Sure, why not?"

"Um . . . I can think of lots of reasons, but if you're up for it, that's great."

"Here you go." Mr. Flanagan handed me his life jacket. "I'm off to score some muffins."

I pulled the life jacket over my head and connected the various snaps and straps.

Spencer started laughing at me.

"What's so funny?" I asked.

"That's a bit large on you." He walked over

to help me adjust it from his dad's size to mine. He put his hand on my waist, cinching the nylon belt.

"Can't you make it any tighter?" I gasped.

"What?"

"I can't breathe!"

"Oh! Sorry." He stepped in closer to make a few adjustments, and I found myself standing eye to cheek-scar. "We just have to make sure it's on there properly in case something happens."

"What's going to happen?" I asked, feeling funny about standing so close with so few clothes on.

"Nothing. A little splash now and then from paddling." He shrugged as he stepped back and got the boat ready for us. "You've kayaked before, right?"

"Sure. Sure." I nodded. "We had a kayak class at camp."

He narrowed his eyes at me. "You went to ballet camp," he said. "Didn't you?"

"Yes, but you can't spend the entire day indoors," I said.

"You can't? Then how do you keep your skin so pale?"

"Through the careful application of sunscreen."

"You could be a member· of Conan O'Brien's Pale Force. They're superheroes who blind people with their paleness," said Spencer.

I frowned at him. "Just get in," I said.

"You first," Spencer offered. I slid into the front seat of the two-person kayak and picked up the paddle. *So far, so good,* I thought. No major incidents, nothing to embarrass me—further—in front of Blake.

"Emily. Emily! Where are you going in that thing?" my mother shouted. "Don't you know this area is known as the Graveyard of the Atlantic?"

"Mom, that's for big boats running aground!" I called over my shoulder. "Not us!"

"Wow." Spencer was just staring at me, holding on to both sides of the kayak.

"What?"

He nodded. "Impressed that you knew that."

"I'm a good tourist. I read all the brochures and signs." I smiled.

"Right." Spencer climbed into the kayak, and, at the same time, pushed off with his back foot. "Now, the thing we have to do is attack the water to get past these first couple waves, okay? So when I say paddle, you really have to paddle."

"Gotcha." I settled into my seat and we took our first paddle. A wave was curling about fifteen feet off, but I knew it would break before it got to us. We paddled on, through its foamy bubbles after it broke, and headed farther out.

I saw another medium-size wave coming, but it was still a ways off. Suddenly, just to my right, I spotted something jump. I watched again. "Look! Over there! Dolphins!"

"Paddle!" Spencer shouted.

"Dolphins—did you see?" I pointed with my paddle.

"*Wave!* Did you see—"

The bow of the kayak went straight up—then the wave crashed right on top of us—and we tipped to the right, completely falling over, getting tumbled and thrown around by the water. The kayak was tilted on its side and I was instantly drenched with water. I half fell, half climbed out.

"Not one of your more graceful moves," Spencer said as he swam and walked back toward shore.

I couldn't stop laughing. "Oh, my God, imagine how dumb that must have looked!"

"Don't worry, I'm sure only about two hundred people were watching, including your boy Blake, and his latest flame—"

"Quiet!" I said, still laughing as a strap from Spencer's life jacket got tangled up in the boat, and he fell into me, knocking me to the sand in the shallow water.

"Okay, apparently you neglected to read the brochure on kayak safety," Spencer began as we clambered to our feet, brushing sand off our swimsuits and legs. "The thing is that you have to get beyond the waves in order to start sightseeing. And when I tell you to paddle—*paddle*!"

"I know, but they were dolphins, Spencer. Real, live dolphins!" I said.

"What's the big deal? Haven't you ever been to SeaWorld?"

"No, and besides, these are wild dolphins. Free range. Whatever," I said. "That makes them so much more interesting. Let's go back out—we have time, don't we, before today's tour of whatever?" I looked at my pink watch. The numbers didn't flash anymore. "My watch!"

"Does that thing actually tell time or does it just beep when the Hello Kitty trend is over, so you know when to throw it out?"

"What? I'd never throw it out, what are you saying?" I looked at it again. "You got your wish. Kitty seems to have drowned. Good-bye Hello Kitty," I said, and we both laughed. "Why is everyone standing on the deck?" I asked. "Are they laughing at us?"

"I would be."

"Why are they waving hysterically at us?"

"Maybe those aren't dolphins," Spencer suggested. "Maybe they're sharks."

"What? No." I shook my head. "Definitely dolphins. Should we try to go out on the water again now or should we ask them what's going on first?"

"My mom's waving at me. We'd better see what it's all about." Spencer pulled the kayak up on the beach, closer to the house, and we laid the paddles underneath it.

I took off my life jacket and draped it over the edge of the deck to dry out, and Spencer did the same.

"What's going on?" I asked as we walked up onto the deck to join the group.

"Linden just called. The admissions office," Adam said. A big grin spread across his face. "I got in!" He picked me up and swung me around. "Isn't that incredible?"

"Congratulations, man." Spencer reached for Adam's hand to shake it, and they did one of those guy-hugs where they pat each other's shoulder and hug without really touching.

"Of course, I'm not that surprised. I knew I was going to get in," Adam said.

"Right. Of course," Spencer teased him.

"Can you believe it? All four of us at the same time?"

"So, you've been saving up?" my dad was asking Mr. Thompson, and they started teasing each other about how much textbooks would cost and how we'd bankrupt them before junior year.

"Now isn't the time to be practical. Let's celebrate! Group hug!" Mrs. Thompson said, and they forced us all into this mob-scene hug.

Everyone was hugging and laughing and the twins were shrieking, and I just stood there with my cheek crushed against Spencer's chest, thinking, *Boy, this feels kind of nice. And oh, no, this college deal is going to be awkward. I am really starting to like Spencer. Again. Or, rather, still. Maybe even more than the last time I saw him. And we're all so close. If I try to say anything again, and I blow it, we'll all be at the same school. And I'll want to transfer.*

But if I don't say anything and he goes out with someone else, I'll be completely miserable and I'll want to transfer.

I was stuck.

Chapter 13

"You know what would be great? If you all ended up in the same dorm," Heather's mom said.

We were having a big dinner to celebrate the news that Adam had gotten into Linden. All the parents had prepared it together, and we had clams, shrimp, steak, three different salads, and enough veggies, chips, and dips to feed an army.

"If you were in the same dorm, then the guys would be right there to look after you, keep an eye on you for us," Mrs. Olsen continued.

"Oh, that would be nice," my mom agreed, nodding.

"I can look after Heather," I piped in, feeling

completely full from the last stuffed shrimp I'd eaten.

"Yeah. And I don't want to burst your bubble, but Adam's going to be too busy doing sports, and Spencer wouldn't do that at all," Heather said.

"He wouldn't? What do you mean?" Her mom looked surprised.

"Well, he pretty much only cares about Spencer."

Spencer looked over at us with an exaggerated, clown-like sad face. *"Me?"*

"That's not true. He volunteered for months," my mother said, coming to his defense. "He's given up a year of the most exciting time in a young person's life to help others."

"Wait a minute, Mrs. Matthias. Are you saying I can't get it back?" Spencer asked, looking puzzled. "That year is like, gone?"

I wanted to laugh, but at the same time I didn't want him to think he was funny. Is that selfish?

"Spencer, tell me about your year off," my dad said. "I'd love to hear more about that.

What was the coolest thing about volunteering?"

"Meeting all the people. Amazing people. A lot more interesting than us, you know? Different lives. Some of them have been through so much, lost everything, and they're still positive," he said. "Which is incredible to me."

"Okay, so we're impressed by the way he helps total strangers," Heather said to the group. "But he doesn't associate with us . . . unless he has to. He already told us he wasn't even going to talk to us at Linden."

"What?" Spencer cried. "I never said that—"

"You did." I nodded.

"I wasn't serious! I was just giving you a hard time," Spencer said. "Come on, guys."

"I heard him, too," Adam said. "Plus, he gave me a hard time about not getting in."

"My apologies. To all of you," Spencer said.

I glanced over at Heather's plate and saw she hadn't eaten much, even though everyone else was completely pigging out on the delicious food. I wondered if she was feeling okay. She hadn't said anything, but she had seemed a little down for most of the night.

"Maybe you can redeem yourself by clearing the table," suggested Spencer's dad.

"Fine." Spencer got up and started taking away empty plates, and I took another look at Heather while our parents continued to plot what would be best for us when we got to college. I was starting to think they all needed to go back to school for advanced degrees—for any kind of degree. Just not at Linden.

"Are you done?" Spencer asked Heather, gesturing to her plate.

"For now. I'll eat leftovers later," she said.

"What's great about Linden is that it's a small campus, but you still meet people from all over the world," Mr. Thompson was saying.

"Oh, sure, but you have to sign up for activities, clubs—" my dad chimed in. "In fact, tell you what. First thing you do when you hit campus is go to the Linden Leadership Office."

"Actually, I think I'll find my dorm room first," Adam said with a laugh, looking over at me and Heather, as if to say, *Help! I can't take any more advice!*

Heather poked my leg. "Are you with me?" she whispered.

"What?" I whispered back.

"Just follow me!" Heather gestured to Adam and Spencer, too.

As the adults continued to talk about their best moves in college, Heather grabbed cups and a half-full bottle of white wine from the table, and the four of us sprinted for the stairs.

"Hey! Where are you—" my mother sputtered.

"We need to plot our own strategy, have our own celebration," I told her. "We'll be back, don't worry!"

We hurried outside, across the deck, and down onto the beach. Adam took the bottle of wine from Heather and started filling our cups. Then he set the bottle in the sand, grinding the bottom down a little so it wouldn't fall over and spill.

"Look out, I think you just killed something," Spencer said, holding something up to the slim moonlight.

Adam stared at it. "It's a shell."

"A shell of its former self, that's what it is," Spencer said. "This is a sand crab, and this little sand crab is part of a community, and—"

Adam groaned. "Listen up, Al Gore. We're trying to have fun here." He took a sip from his cup. "Okay? So don't mention how the tide is too high and the beach is eroding and we're killing all the sand life."

"Fine. I won't. But we are." Spencer drained the rest of his cup of wine, then grabbed the bottle for a refill.

Heather sank onto the sand beside me and stretched her legs, then scrunched up into a ball, hugging her knees. She took a sip of wine. She didn't seem to be in that celebrating mood we were all supposed to be in, and I wondered if the big, special dinner was making the adults happier than it was making us—and her, in particular.

"Great night," I said. "I mean, weather."

"Hmm," Heather agreed.

"So. I'm totally not trying to pry, but . . . how are things?" I asked. "Besides Dean, because we know things are going great there." I smiled.

"Okay." She sighed. "I guess."

"Are you sure?" I asked.

"It's just . . . some days are hard. I mean, it's been an incredibly hard year. I think that's why I want to unwind so much while I'm here, with you and everyone," she said. "It just feels really good to get away from there. From home, I mean."

"I can imagine," I said. "Sort of. I'm sure I don't know anything, though."

"At home there are lots of memories. I've never been here before, so . . ." She shrugged. "Despite the fact I have to hang out with all of my dad's best friends, it's actually okay. Then I think about going home."

"You won't be there too long," I said.

"True. But then we'll go to Linden. And Dad was all about Linden. You know?" she asked.

I nodded. "He'd be really proud of you, knowing you're going."

She squeezed her cup, crumpling it a bit. "But he's supposed to *be* there at Homecoming."

"I know. Totally embarrassing you by

wearing a giant Linden sweatshirt with a matching hat, and shouting through a megaphone—"

"Yeah," Heather said. "Exactly."

Spencer sat down on the other side of her. "Now you'll just have to listen to Emily's dad singing the leaf song."

"It's not the leaf song," I protested. "It's called 'Linden, My Linden.'"

"Listen to her. Trying to suck up already by knowing the school song," Spencer said.

"You guys. It's not funny. It's not fair," Heather said quietly. I looked at her and saw a tear sliding down her cheek.

"It isn't fair," I agreed, "you're right."

"Completely unfair," Spencer agreed.

"It sucks, is what," said Adam as the four of us gathered in a semicircle.

Heather sat there for a minute, just quietly crying, resting her chin on her arms. I had put my arm around her, and Spencer put his arm around her, too. I didn't know what I could say.

"You know what, Heather?" Spencer said. "I really wanted to be there, for the memorial service. I only saw your dad a couple times a year, but he made a big impression on me."

"He did?"

"Yeah." Spencer nodded. "You know how my dad can be hard on me sometimes? Like, he thinks I should be exactly like him, and I'm not. Well, your dad must have noticed that, and he'd always find a way to tell me it was cool, whatever I decided to be. 'Football isn't life,' he said once, when my dad was criticizing my passing technique."

"Which you have to admit, sucks," Adam noted.

"Anyway, I just thought you should know—we all miss him, too. And we're not going to forget him," Spencer said.

"Thanks." Heather sniffled.

"When that happened . . . the real reason I couldn't come to the funeral was I had this really close friend—from high school. He got hit by a car, riding his bike off campus. It was the day before we were supposed to fly out and he was in a coma. I couldn't just leave him."

"Did he die?" I finally asked.

"No, but he was unconscious for a week, then he couldn't walk for months. His memory's still not all there. He's just getting out of rehab now, and . . . anyway. It's not about him. I mean, it's about—you find yourself walking around wondering what's the point? Because it *isn't* fair."

"Exactly," Heather said.

"And you have no idea what's coming, but all of a sudden your whole life can change. That's not fair, either," Spencer went on. "I can't even begin to imagine how much worse it is for you. We all miss your dad, but that's not even—a millionth of it."

I watched him just holding Heather, letting her collapse against him.

Suddenly, he seemed like the best and nicest friend a person could have.

I didn't just want to be in the same dorm with him. I wanted to be *with* him, with him.

"You know what we'll have to do," Adam said. "We'll have to all take off together some weekend. Go camping. Just get away from campus."

"Camping?" Heather scoffed. "How about a hotel? In Detroit or someplace. Or Los Angeles, maybe. Ooh—what about Mexico?"

"Are you talking about spring break? Already?" teased Spencer.

"What's wrong with camping?" Adam asked.

I cleared my throat. "Remember the night we all slept outside? By that cabin in New Hampshire? And a porcupine decided to try and sneak into the tent?"

"*What* tent?" Spencer said.

"Oh, yeah. *That* was the problem." Adam started to laugh. "And you—Heather—you tried to fend him off with your hair dryer—you brought your hair dryer camping—"

"And you threw a book at it—and missed, thank God—"

"Remember, Emily?" Spencer was holding his stomach. "You said, 'p-p-p-p-p-' for like ten minutes before you could get the word *porcupine* out."

We were all laughing so hard, it was impossible to talk. *Must be the wine,* I thought. Heather seemed happier, which was really all I cared about.

"Em?" Spencer knocked on my door. "You in there?"

I was half undressed, toweling off my hair. We'd all run into the ocean for a late-night swim after our little wine party, and then we'd headed inside to change into dry clothes. I quickly pulled on a clean T-shirt, a dry pair of jeans, and opened the door.

"I think I got your fleece jacket by mistake. It's a small-medium and I haven't worn a small-medium since eighth grade." He handed me my jacket and walked past me into the room.

"You were really short back then," I observed.

"Thank you. I remember it well."

"I didn't know you could climb four flights without passing out," I teased him.

"I've been training." Spencer wandered around the room. "So this is what it's like to have the best room in the house."

"It's not the best—look how small it is," I pointed out.

"Look how private it is," Spencer countered. "Look how your parents are not sleeping in the living room."

"That's only because there *is* no living room."

"But you're all alone. What if you wake up in the middle of the night, crying? Your parents won't be there."

"Shut up," I said, shoving him so that he fell onto my bed.

He put his hands behind his head and bounced a few times on the bed. "Your bed is more comfortable than mine," he complained. "You have way more room up here than I do." Then he jumped up and went out to the balcony. "So this is what I look like from up here."

"Like what?" I asked, walking out beside him. The last time I'd stood on this balcony with anyone, it had been Blake. The balcony had a sort of jinxed feeling, like maybe if we stood here too long, we'd plummet to the ground.

"Um . . . short. I guess." Spencer shrugged.

"So . . . when we were all talking, earlier, on the beach? There was something I wanted to say. But I couldn't tell everyone, but maybe I can tell you."

"Okay," I said slowly. "Go ahead."

"I have a confession to make. And I'm only going to tell you. I mean, eventually I'll have to tell everyone, or everyone will find out, anyway, but maybe for now we could sort of keep it between us. Okay?"

"Sure," I said with a smile, but I was afraid to ask. Afraid to find out. What if it was something extremely private? What if it was "I'm gay"? What if it was "I'm in love with Heather"?

"What is it?" I finally asked, after running through all the worst-case scenarios in my mind.

"The reason I know so much about freshman orientation? I already went through it," he said.

"You what?"

"I went through it already," Spencer said. "I started college last year."

"You did? Where? But you said—"

"I didn't stay long enough to finish the semester, so it doesn't count. We don't talk about it much, because my folks were so mad at me, because they spent the money."

"Okay. Explain," I said.

"I didn't want to go to Linden, because I was so sick of being pressured to apply there by my dad. I mean, I applied and I got in, but I applied other places, too, and at the last minute I decided to start at UVM instead of Linden. It was a lot less expensive, closer to home, and most of all—it was the opposite of what my dad wanted. A bigger school, and *not* Linden. I don't know if you know this. But my dad and I have this history of me trying to live up to what he wants—and it isn't what I want."

"I know a little about that," I said. "So what happened?"

"I went to UVM, but I didn't really want to be there. Nothing against the school—it just wasn't the right fit for me. There was that thing with my good friend getting hurt, so I was home a lot visiting him, and I didn't know how to deal with living in a dorm, I didn't like my classes—everything was just wrong."

"Maybe because the guys talk up Linden so much—like college is supposed to be *so* amazing," I said. "Anything less than that and you probably feel like you're missing out, or doing something wrong."

"Exactly!"

Spencer's eyes were shining in the small amount of light that came from my room. I'd never seen him so animated—it was like we were really connecting over this. I hadn't even had time to process what he'd just told me— that his time off had ended up being for a good cause, but that he hadn't started out exactly with that noble plan in mind.

"So, you left? You just . . . up and left in the middle of the semester? Wow. That's . . . gutsy," I told him.

"Not really." He shook his head. "I didn't know what to do. I didn't want to sit around at home, I knew that. And our community center and church were organizing this trip. I went for the two weeks, and then I just stayed. And stayed. After a while I realized how lucky I was, how I had all these chances to make my life be whatever I wanted. So I called and talked to the admissions counselor at Linden, and they let me reapply. And that is the long, boring story of why I'll be a freshomore."

"It wasn't boring," I said.

"No?" he asked.

"Well. Not nearly as boring as your girl-next-door story, anyway," I said.

"What?" he cried. "Hey, I only *told* you that because I felt sorry for you—"

"Well, it worked, because afterward I felt sorry for *you*."

We were laughing when there was a loud knock and suddenly Heather barged into the room.

"Oh, my God, you have to see this. The guys are all competing to see who can make the biggest splash in the pool—and my mom's videotaping. They're making total idiots of themselves—Spencer, your dad is winning! Come on!"

Spencer and I bumped into each other on the way off the balcony. Then we both tried to squeeze through the door at the same time.

"After you," Spencer said, holding out his hand to show me the way.

"No, after you," I said.

I felt closer to Spencer tonight than I ever had before. The problem was, what was I going to do about it *this* time?

Something? Anything? Nothing?

When we got downstairs, Heather was greeting Dean with a hug at the door to the pool area. Spencer and I waited to say hi to him, and just before Dean closed the door behind him, Blake stepped up out of the shadows. "What's going on, y'all? Sounds fun."

"Actually, it's a private party," Spencer told him. "Sorry. No Neanderthals allowed."

"No what?" asked Blake.

"Exactly. 'Night, y'all. Safety first." Spencer closed the door in his face.

I laughed, feeling almost as satisfied as if I'd

been the one to dis him. "Thanks."

"No prob. We've got enough Neanderthals in here already." He pointed to his dad, who was about to do a cannonball off the diving board. "Run for cover!"

Chapter 14

The next morning we toured Kitty Hawk, for our Mom-influenced group activity. After lunch, Heather and I took off on a shopping spree. Well, as much of a spree as a person can have with only $45 in her pocket. I also wanted to spend time with her and make sure she was doing okay after last night. She was so strong and resilient. I really admired her for that, in the midst of our silly vacation stuff.

"This is great. We can meet Chase and Dean tonight for a late swim, then go to dinner—"

"Actually, um, Heather? I appreciate everything you're doing. But I'm not interested in Chase."

"How do you know? You've barely talked to him."

"The thing is . . . I think I'm interested in someone else."

"Not Blake. Still."

I shook my head. "No, not Blake."

"Phew. Then who?"

"Don't laugh, okay?"

"Why would I laugh?"

"Because it's Spencer," I said.

Heather giggled, then put her hand over her mouth. "Sorry. Not laughing. Because you're apparently . . . serious. You like *Spencer*?" she cried.

"Shh! Do you have to tell the entire store? What if he's in here?"

"Why would he be in here?"

"He's been known to follow us. Remember?"

"True. But I doubt that he'd set foot in Brenda's Bikini World."

I giggled. "Well, no, unless he was trying to meet girls." Then that thought sort of made me feel sick.

"You know, he was really great last night when I got upset. That was like a whole other side of him."

"I know. I feel like I've been getting to know him pretty well. Despite the fact he has this whole layer of arrogance. And I just . . . I find that I want to get even closer to him. Does that sound dumb? That sounds dumb."

"It sounds kind of sexy, if you ask me. So, is that why we're here?"

"Why we're where?" I asked.

"At this shop! Because you plan to make your move wearing something sexy?"

"No! We're in this shop because you dragged me in here. Anyway, I don't even know how to make a so-called move. I don't make 'moves.' I make . . . mistakes," I said.

Heather laughed. "But see, that's where you're wrong. So you're not the type of person to just have a meaningless fling. That's great. I totally support that. You're more about the long-term relationship."

I held up a red, flowered strapless top. "Then how come I've never *had* one?"

"You were waiting for the right person."

"No, I was waiting. Period."

"What do you mean?"

"Well, whenever I've liked a guy, I've always waited too long to tell them how I feel. And then before I say anything, they end up moving away, leaving town, or even worse, hooking up with someone else."

"So. That isn't going to happen with Spencer. But it could, when we get to college. So don't wait any longer. Tell him."

"It sounds so simple. You know? When you say it, I can picture doing it. But when it comes down to making it happen, I can't."

"You know what? This totally makes sense. He likes you, too. I mean, why did he butt in where Blake was concerned? Why does he constantly give you a hard time—"

"He gives everyone a hard time," I reminded her.

"Please. He doesn't want you to be with anyone else because he wants you."

As much as I loved the thought of that, I wondered if it was just wishful thinking.

Friends did that a lot for each other.

"He's into you. Trust me," Heather said.

"Why? Did he say anything to you?" I asked, feeling hopeful, wishing there was some sort of evidence that I could cling to so I'd feel more confident if I ever did go to him.

"No, but I can tell by the way he was looking at you last night. When I came into your room? Wait. Did I interrupt something?"

"No. Not exactly." I felt my face turn red. "Maybe. I don't know! He's so hard to read. Which is funny, considering all he *does* is read. That should make him transparent, don't you think? The thing is, I find it totally impossible to talk to guys. To tell them how I feel. So, what I was thinking was, how about if I just write him a letter? Slip it under his door?"

"Emily." She gave me a very serious look. "I know it's very hard. And really intimidating. But one thing to remember is you don't ever write a letter telling them."

I knew I should probably trust Heather on this. She had the rules: You get a guy's name and number. You let him know you're interested. "No? Letters don't work?"

"By the time he gets and reads the letter he could be hooking up with someone else."

"Really? But what if we're, like, meant to be?" I asked.

"What if someone else reads it? Or what if he shows it to other people?" She shook her head. "Oh, no. Trust me on this. Never write anything down. Don't even send a text or e-mail. It'll be retrieved from his computer one day and you'll die of embarrassment," she said.

"Okay. Well. I could do a photo collage, then. A story in pictures," I said. "I could show this progression—hold on, I could make a *movie*—"

"Emily, how long is *that* going to take? Two weeks? You don't have two weeks."

"I know, but what about Linden? I mean, what about the fact we're both going there—isn't this a horrible, terrible idea?" I asked.

"You're looking for excuses. Who cares about Linden? Get him alone. And tell him. And go try that on." Heather pointed to the eensy-weensy bikini I'd been examining.

"Are you sure?"

"What's the point of staying in shape and doing all that dancing if you don't show it off?"

"Well, the thing is, once I put this on, I don't think I'll be able to *move*," I said. "Without it falling off."

"Hey, no problem—that could really speed things along," she joked.

I stuck out my tongue at her as I swept the changing-room curtain closed. I'd brought in some other suits, too. I wasn't the type to be sexy by revealing everything—I needed something a little more modest, or I'd be so self-conscious I wouldn't be able to talk to anyone—or even leave my room.

When we got home, I put on my new bikini, slipped into a pair of pink nylon board shorts and my flip-flops, and went to find Spencer. I was feeling very charged up from the two coffees I'd had during our shopping spree, like I could accomplish anything.

He was sitting in the third-floor living room, reading yet another classic novel, right where I'd left him earlier.

What do I do now? I wondered. *He's alone. We're alone. I could slide onto the sofa next to him and just . . . tell him.*

But then the image of the last time I tried this popped into my brain. Me, lying on the floor in a sleeping bag, at the condo we'd rented. Spencer, sitting on a fold-out sofa. Me, getting up and sitting next to him, telling him how I felt, how I thought he was cool, how I wished we could see each other more often. And other embarrassing, personal things like that.

Him, interrupting me, changing the subject, saying anything except, "Yeah, I feel the same way about *you*." Saying something about "I have to get some sleep," and disappearing under a blanket, his back to me.

What was I doing this for? Did I *enjoy* torture?

"Hey, Spencer. You want to go out in the kayak?" I asked, perching on the edge of the chair opposite him.

He looked over at me. "Not really."

"Come on. Please?"

He stretched his arms over his head and yawned. "I thought you hated water sports, and sports of any kind."

"Yeah, but I had a good time kayaking. Remember?"

"You fell *out* of the kayak."

Oops. "True. But I'm an excellent swimmer," I said. "Plus, I want to take some pictures out there. Find some dolphins again."

"You can't just find them. It's not like a whale watch. I mean, they don't have schedules."

"They don't?" I gasped, putting my hand over my mouth.

He laughed. "Okay, so we'll look for dolphins, but no crying if we don't find any."

"Like I'd cry. Have you ever seen me cry?"

"Please. I was there when your dad had to tie a string to one of your front baby teeth and pull it out. You cried."

"Oh. Well. Hopefully none of my teeth are going to fall out."

"And how about the time we went to that amusement park—and your cotton candy fell off the stick? Major tears."

"Can you blame me?" I asked as I followed him down the stairs.

He stopped walking, and I crashed into him. "What do you mean, you want to go out there and take pictures? You're bringing your camera after what happened last time? Do you not remember getting soaked?"

"Give me some credit. Don't worry, I have a waterproof, disposable one. Ten bucks and it floats." I took it out of my shorts pocket to show him.

"Well. As long as *we* float, too, that should work."

We grabbed the life jackets from the first floor and pulled the kayak down from where it leaned against the deck stairs, toward the water.

When we got in, I wished we'd capsize. Sink. Anything to give me an easy opening like, *Please don't sink because I like you! I'm drowning! I need mouth-to-mouth resuscitation!*

I didn't know how to tell him, what I was supposed to say. The way we sat in the kayak, his back was already turned to me, because he'd insisted on switching around this time. That didn't bode well.

"Lovely weather, isn't it?" I commented.

"Sure," he said.

"Ooh! Is that a dolphin?" I pointed out into the ocean at something sort of gray.

"That's a bird, floating," Spencer said.

"Oh." I kept paddling, making sure we stayed parallel to the coastline and didn't go too far out. I could swim, but not in a triathlon sort of way. "You know what? Birds are cool. Coastal birds. The way they just hover and then dive for the kill." *Maybe I could strive to be more like them*, I thought with a smile.

Spencer didn't respond. I didn't blame him. He was paddling very weakly as if he didn't care whether we got anywhere or not.

"You know what else is cool? The Outer Banks," I said. "Talk about a gem."

"What are you, the Chamber of Commerce now? You're taking this good tourist—bad tourist thing to extremes."

"Fine. I'll stop talking," I said.

"Great," Spencer replied.

I kept my mouth closed for a minute or two.

But that wasn't the point of this ocean journey. If Spencer didn't want to talk, that was too bad—I had to make him talk. "Don't mind me. I'll just be taking some underwater photos back here. Ooh, look, a coral reef. An octopus. Buried treasure!" I cried. "No *way*!"

Spencer's neck turned ever so slowly to the right and he lowered his new sunglasses to give me an aggravated look. "Do you mind? I'm trying to read."

"What? You're not *reading*," I said.

He held his book over his head to show me.

"I hate you sometimes," I said.

"I know."

I glared at his back. "I hope we're not in any of the same classes."

"I know."

Suddenly, I realized that drinking two large coffees before going out on the ocean in a kayak was not such a great idea. "Since you're not really into it, why don't we just turn back," I suggested. Strongly.

"I'm into it," he said. "I'm just trying to multi-task."

"Well, uh, I actually need to get back. I forgot that I planned to meet Heather," I said.

"Heather can wait."

"No, um, she can't." I awkwardly tried to turn the kayak around. "Little help?"

Later that afternoon, I thought about asking Spencer out for dinner, but he had already gone out with his parents.

When he got back, I challenged him to a game of pool, but the adults were playing, involved in some major challenge, with men versus women.

By the time it was ten at night and I still hadn't managed to say a real, actual word to Spencer in private, I decided that I had no choice. I knew he'd gone to his room earlier to read, but I didn't want to go through his parents' room. Again. I didn't want to watch a game with his dad or apply a facial with his mom. Small talk was out of the question; this was all about the Big Talk.

I stood on my balcony in my bare feet. I peered down at the railing on his. It wasn't that far down. I couldn't calculate how many feet, exactly, but I was hoping no more than five feet and five inches—my body length.

This was the perfect assignment for me. I was limber. I knew how to leap. I could pirouette in midair. Sure, not all these skills were relevant to the task, but I thought about them, anyway, to build my confidence.

In my bare feet, black yoga pants, and T-shirt, I stepped out onto my balcony. I put one foot over the railing, making contact with the edging. I pulled my other leg over, so that I was gripping the edge of my balcony with my toes. I grabbed the bars on the balcony railing and pushed off with my feet, lowering myself and also trying to swing to the left toward Spencer's balcony.

It took me about six swinging attempts to get my feet anywhere near the railing of his balcony. Finally, I made contact and wrapped my left toes around the metal. My right foot was stretched out in the other direction. It was sort of like doing a split in midair—something Heather might do in gymnastics.

I kicked my foot at the railing, trying to get a better grip, trying to swing the rest of my body closer.

Naturally, there was a pop can on the railing I hadn't seen. It clattered onto the balcony floor.

Seconds later, the door to the balcony opened.

Spencer's eyes went from the can to my foot to my suspended body. My upper body was killing me by this point.

"Is there a fire in your room?" he asked.

"No."

"What are you doing out here?"

"Stretching?" I said. Then I coughed, racking my brain for an excuse. "Well, see, I was trying to get a certain shot. Of the moon."

Spencer looked up into the sky, beyond me. "It's cloudy tonight."

"Well, sure it is now, but earlier—anyway, I was trying to get a shot and I fell. Could you just help me down, or up, or something?"

Mr. Flanagan was inside watching a base-ball game, and he and Spencer came over to rescue me, pulling me in by taking hold of my legs.

I didn't want to stick around and get teased. I didn't want to talk about it, period. I just took the muscle-relaxant foot cream Mrs. Flanagan gave me and traipsed upstairs to my room, feeling hopeless.

I'd tried—more than tried—all day. If he couldn't tell what I was trying to do and say, and if I could never manage to say anything meaningful, then I was never going to be able to communicate it to him. He didn't seem to be dying to say anything to *me*, so maybe he didn't feel the same way. But Heather thought he was into me. . . . Was he?

I'd have to rent one of those planes that flew over the beaches, pulling advertising signs behind them. I could manage to get him onto the deck at a certain time, spell it out for him:

SPENCER, YOU IDIOT. CAN'T YOU TELL THAT I LIKE YOU?

That would be too long.

SPENCER. U R THE 1.

No, too stupid.

How about: SPENCER, I'VE BEEN TRYING TO

TELL YOU SOMETHING, BUT BEFORE I DO, COULD YOU TELL ME SOMETHING FIRST, BECAUSE THEN I WON'T STRESS SO MUCH? DEAL?

But what if he didn't want to tell me anything?

Chapter 15

"*H*ow much longer do we have to wait?"

My dad checked his watch and peered at the ferry schedule clutched in his hand. "Half an hour? They run every half hour, and I think we'll fit on the next one, don't you?"

"Hard to say, since we didn't fit on the last two," Adam complained. He was in charge of his twin brothers for the day while his parents enjoyed a day on their own, and he'd been having a hard time keeping them entertained while we waited for the ferry. The thing they found most entertaining was running around the van, then around the Rustbucket (we'd driven two cars so we could split up, if need be), then running to the water's edge and looking like they were about to dive in, and then knocking on other people's car windows. Adam more than had his hands full looking after them, and we'd all been helping out, rescuing them from various disasters in the making.

Our two cars were now only third and fourth in our line, but there were several lines that waited beside us to board the ferry. We'd definitely moved up to the front, but I wasn't sure we were close enough to catch the next boat to Ocracoke Island. Each ferry was only big enough for thirty cars. We'd been warned by my mom to leave early in the morning, but we hadn't—and now we were stuck waiting with the crowd. The ferry took about forty minutes according to my mom's travel book—and it was free, which might have explained why so many people were making the trip.

I thought about how much things had changed since the day I'd run into Blake in the supermarket and he'd told me he was coming to see the island. We'd shared a kiss by the canned peach pyramids. What might have happened if I'd ditched my mom and told Blake I was coming along? That I'd rather fiesta with him than cook a fiesta meal with my mom?

I'd probably be disinherited by now, but maybe things would have worked out with Blake.

No, probably not, I thought. We'd have gotten to the ferry, and then I'd have found out that the red-haired girl was meeting Blake on the island. And I'd have been stranded here on the street, which would have been much worse than being dissed in the middle of a loud club. Even if the music sucked.

Spencer tapped my shoulder. "What are you smiling about?"

"Nothing," I said. "I was actually thinking something really bad."

"Huh." He didn't inquire about the details, which was just as well. "I'm thinking of something bad, too. Like the fact the day is already half over. Do you think the long wait for the ferry is really worth it? We could kayak there faster."

"Did you *bring* the kayak?" I asked.

"Spence, it's worth the wait," Spencer's dad

assured us. "Don't you want to get out on the water?"

"And see where Blackbeard met his fate?" my dad added.

"Yo-ho-ho and a bottle of rum," Heather said. She glanced at her watch. "Are we ever going to get there?"

I sighed. "I'm going to get a pop over there in the visitor center—anyone else want one?"

"I'll come with," Heather said, and we headed for the vending machines inside the building. "Why didn't your mom come? She's always got the cooler full of drinks for us. I was counting on her." She fed two dollar bills into the pop machine.

"She said she wasn't feeling all that well." I shrugged. "What about your mom?"

"She just wanted some time by herself to read and reflect, she said. Personally, I think they're hitting a day spa together," Heather said. "Your mom's the tourist extraordinaire. Why would she miss an item on her list?"

"I know, it's strange," I said. "Maybe she just felt like staying home and making a new list. We've got all next week to fill up with tours and events, remember?"

"We do, that's true." We walked over and stood by the door, looking outside, enjoying the cool air-conditioning. "So. You didn't tell him yet, did you?" Heather asked.

"Not exactly," I replied. *Not this year,* I thought, wondering if I should finally tell Heather how this had gone for me the last time I had attempted it. Badly.

"When are you going to do it?" she pressed.

"I saw you last night! Do you really think I had time between now and then?" I asked her, laughing.

"At least twelve hours," she said. "And it's only going to take you like five minutes. What are you waiting for? Look at him over there. He's pacing around waiting for you to get back."

"Is he? I think he's just impatient for the boat."

"The boat—and *you.*" She pressed my arm with her finger. "Exactly."

I rolled my eyes. "I love the spin you put on

things, but I can't do it. Just thinking about it makes me want to throw up."

"Nah, that's just worrying about being on the boat. Telling him will not be as hard as you think."

"I already have a bruised knee and a questionable hamstring muscle," I said, "from trying to be Catwoman last night."

"Well, I didn't tell you to scale *buildings*," she said, and we laughed. After my disastrous attempts, I'd called Heather—she was just on her way home from seeing a movie with Dean, and we'd gotten together for ice cream in my room to laugh about it.

"I thought it was a brilliant idea," I said. "And it could have worked."

"Could have," Heather agreed. "But why don't you just try sitting next to him on the ferry and telling him? Might be a little less risky."

"With everyone else around?" I scoffed. "No way. That would be so embarrassing."

"It isn't easy. I know. Okay, I'll give you a hint."

"It better be a big one," I said. "I need all the help I can get."

"Shut up. You're constantly saying that and putting yourself down. You did fine meeting Blake. It just didn't work out, that's all."

"Well, that's sort of the truth," I said with a laugh.

"Anyway. What I usually do? Is give myself a deadline."

"A deadline?" I asked. "What kind of deadline?"

"Tell yourself that you're not leaving the island, or ending today, without telling him how you feel, that he's the Spencerest of all the Spencers you know, or whatever."

"Whatever I say? It's going to be better than that," I assured her as we both cracked up. "Wait a second. Did you just say today?" I nearly dropped my pop can on my foot. "Are you insane?"

"No," she said. "Do you want to spend the rest of your vacation pining away for him or do you want to start hanging out? And making out?"

"But what if I bomb like last time?"

"What last time?"

As we waited, I finally told her the story of what had happened when I was fifteen, and how Spencer had completely blown off my attempt to get closer to him.

Although it had been horribly embarrassing for me, she didn't seem fazed in the slightest.

"You know what? I would not feel bad about that at all," Heather scoffed. "I bet he didn't even know you were making a move."

How I wished that were true. "Oh, he knew. He's referred to it once or twice on this trip."

"In a fun way?" she asked.

"Let's see. Is teasing and glaring considered fun? Maybe in *some* cultures."

"That's Spencer, though. I mean, hate to say it, but he's not exactly the warm-and-fuzzy type. He doesn't have a clue about how to talk to people—that's why I told him he'd have to brush up on his socials skills—or should I say *skill*, because he doesn't have more than one—before he goes off to Linden and immediately insults a bunch of people."

"He's not that bad," I said.

"Easy for you to say. You're falling for him. Or you already fell, actually," she said. "Off your balcony."

"Great. I'm going to be teased about this for life, aren't I?" I said. Outside, my dad was waving his arms in the air, trying to get our attention. He pointed at the ocean, then at the car, then at us. I waved to let him know we got the message.

"Pretty much," Heather said as we hurried over to the car. A ferry was just docking, and everyone was starting their engines again, preparing to board. "Don't worry. We'll find something else soon."

"That's so reassuring," I said as we climbed into the Rustbucket.

"What's reassuring?" Spencer asked, turning around in the front seat, where he sat beside my dad, who was driving.

"Hold on. Here we go, kids!" My dad started humming the tune to the very old TV show, *Gilligan's Island*, where the characters were on a three-hour boat tour and got stranded on an island for a few seasons.

"Dad. We're not going out in some small fishing boat," I said.

"Neither was Gilligan, Em. Neither was Gilligan." And there he was, driving us onto the ferry, singing the theme song at the top of his lungs.

Somewhere, the world was missing a very strange accountant.

Maybe he needed to take more vacation days.

Four hours later, we'd had a delicious late lunch at a café right on the harbor, seen the Ocracoke Lighthouse, the pirate museum, the place where Blackbeard was said to have met his fate. We'd also seen houses, gift shops, art studios, and the tiniest cemetery I'd ever seen, which was for four British soldiers killed during World War II. We'd done almost everything as a tight-knit group, so I hadn't had a minute alone with Spencer—in fact, we'd both spent lots of time holding on to or chasing Tim and Tyler.

We'd gone back to the visitor center in the middle of town, where we'd parked, so Adam could get some snacks for the kids out of the van. "Hey, my dad just called—there's some bad weather coming in—thunderstorms—and he was thinking I really should get the boys home at a semi-decent hour, so we need to head back."

"That's probably a good idea," said my dad. "We don't want to be out here in the middle of a storm."

"It's a really good idea," Heather agreed.

"Okay. We'll all go, I guess." I looked at Heather and shrugged.

"Yes. But we have the two cars," my dad said. "So you don't need to rush off."

"Yes. Really," Heather said. "You guys stay. Enjoy the local flavors. Go shopping!"

"No thanks, I'm done shopping," said Spencer. He turned to me. "You?"

"I'm broke," I said. "But maybe I should stay a little while and try to get some nighttime pictures."

"Well, you can't stay here by yourself. Who

would like to stay and keep Emily company? How about you, Spencer?" my dad suggested.

"Yeah, sure. That's probably a good idea. What about you, Heather? You want to stay, too?" Spencer asked.

"Oh, I—I can't," she said. "I need to go check in with my mom and see how she's doing." Heather came closer and pulled me aside. "Listen, Emily. Don't you see—this is the perfect opportunity. I can't stay—I'm supposed to be meeting Dean tonight, so I've got to head back. But you and Spencer can stay, together."

"You're ditching me?" I asked.

"Did you tell him yet?" Heather asked.

"No . . ." I said slowly. "Do long looks at him count?"

She threw up her hands. "Then I'm definitely ditching you. What are you waiting for? Tell him."

"Give me a break! I haven't had a chance."

"Right. Sure you haven't," Heather said. "Well, you're definitely going to have a chance now."

"Okay. How should I—"

"Emily, you're smart. You'll think of something."

I raised my right eyebrow, daring her to leave me. What was this, tough love? She calmly walked over and climbed into the van, where Tim and Tyler were already buckled in and waiting. Adam got in beside her, then my dad got in, taking the driver's seat, looking like a chauffeur. Spencer's mom and dad were the last ones in.

"Call to check in!" Mr. Flanagan yelled over his shoulder, his voice mingling with my dad's, who was saying the same exact thing. Then the sliding doors dinged and closed, they pulled away, and Spencer and I were left standing in the parking lot.

"So where did you want to get those pictures?" Spencer asked.

"I was thinking some sunset pictures. By the lighthouse?" I suggested.

"If it weren't cloudy, that would be a great concept." Spencer looked up at the sky. "You didn't want to do that, anyway. Too clichéd."

"How about if I take some pictures of you, then?" I suggested.

"You must have enough to fill three albums and crash the Shutterfly site," he said drily. "You could photograph the storm. How do you feel about pictures of lightning strikes?"

I eyed the darkening sky. "I think they're the kind of weather photos other people should take. You know, maybe we should just go. If we leave now we could meet them at the ferry line."

"Yeah, but if we wait a little, maybe there won't be as much of a line," he argued. "We could grab a bite somewhere and wait out the storm?"

"Sure, okay. Except . . . I don't know. I — don't feel good." That wasn't far from the truth. I was feeling more nervously ill all the time.

He just stared at me, completely unsympathetic. "You were feeling fine ten minutes ago. When you ate that ice cream."

"Well, that's it, maybe it was something I ate, then."

"Are you going to get sick?"

Way to kill any romance, Emily, I thought. *By suggesting nausea.* "No, I just feel a little dizzy. You know, like when you try to read the newspaper in the car and all the lines start waving around and go blurry?"

"That doesn't happen to me."

"Oh."

"Maybe if you read more, you'd get used to reading in the car," Spencer said.

"Ha-ha. Do you really want to insult me when I feel sick?"

"Well, what do you want me to do?"

"Let's walk around some more. I'm sure I'll feel better in a little while."

"How about if we just sit down over there?" Spencer gestured to a picnic table by the water.

"Fine."

Spencer looked at his watch and then at the sky.

"You're contemplating leaving me here, aren't you?"

"No. I just wondered what we should do. We should probably go now, make a run for it, or wait until later. Unless you were thinking we'd spend the night here?" Spencer said.

Thought you'd never ask.

"Because that's absurd," Spencer said. "We

don't have enough money to rent a room, even if there were any vacancies, which I seriously doubt."

"Right. Okay, well, we can go then, I guess." I wasn't very good at stalling. I consoled myself with thinking about the fact we still had the ferry ride back to Hatteras and then the long car trip from there to Kill Devil Hills. I had plenty of time to talk to him. Seriously.

We both got into the Rustbucket sedan and I turned the key. I waited for the inevitable roar, the bleating sound of old, worn-out engine belts, and the mild kicking sound from the exhaust pipe.

There was no sound. At all.

I turned the key again. Nothing.

"Let me try," said Spencer.

"Okay, but why would you be able to start it and I can't?" I asked as I opened the door and got out. Spencer slid into the driver's seat and tried to get it started, but nothing happened then, either.

"I think it's sea-logged," he said. "The rust has taken over."

"Now what?" I asked.

"We could leave the car here overnight and run to the ferry," Spencer suggested.

"It's a long way. And if it rains?"

He tapped his fingers against the steering wheel. "We'll hitch a ride, then," he said.

"People only do that in crime shows. And then they're the opening crime," I said.

"You watch a lot of TV, don't you?" he commented.

"Not really. It's more my mom's thing," I explained. "That's why she has this tendency to worry incessantly. Too many episodes of *Law & Order TDE*."

"TDE?"

"Teen Daughter Edition," I said.

Spencer laughed and opened the driver's door. He got out and we both stood by the car, staring at it, willing it to work . . . wishing somebody would happen to drop by with a tow truck.

"I still say we have to give it a shot. We don't have to hitchhike exactly, we can just go over to the place where we had lunch and see if anyone's headed—"

There was a crack of thunder and it was as if a cloud directly over our heads opened up and dumped out all the moisture inside—right onto us. We both shrieked and jumped back into the car—me in the driver's seat, and Spencer right behind me.

We laughed as we tried to roll up the windows as water seemed to stream into the car from all directions.

Then we sat there, safe inside, and listened to the crashes and booms outside, watching water stream down the windows.

I peeked over the back of my headrest at Spencer. I could tell him how much I liked him right now, but then what? We were stuck in a car in the middle of a thunderstorm. Running away would not be fun—or easy. Or survivable.

The windows were starting to get steamed up, but not for any exciting reasons.

"I'd better, uh, call my dad," I said. "Tell him what happened, where we are. Or aren't."

Spencer nodded. "Good idea. I should check in with my folks, too."

I quickly told my dad what had happened,

and while they were already heading home on the ferry, he said he'd call my mom to tell her what was going on and see what she could do to help. I think I interrupted him from singing everyone else in the van—or at least Tyler and Tim—to sleep.

"Okay. So we've checked in. Now what?" Spencer asked.

"Should we stay here, sleep in the car? It'd be cheap. Uncomfortable, but cheap," I said. "I think these seats recline."

Spencer eyed me and then the seats. "Let's look at that as our worst-case scenario."

I glanced over at him. *Thanks. Thanks a lot*, I thought. "It's not like I desperately wanted to spend the night with you, either," I said. "I mean, uh, spend the night in a car with my neck all bent funny and nowhere to brush my teeth and no pillow and—"

"It's cool. I know what you meant."

"You do?" I was about to say something like, *No, I don't think you do, actually*.

My phone rang—it was my mom. Saving me, thank goodness. "Emily, before you say anything, just tell me you're all right," she said, which is never a good start to a conversation, but which is fairly typical for her.

"Mom. I'm perfectly fine," I said.

"We called the Rustbucket Repair number, and unfortunately, they don't send out repair vehicles at night. But someone will be there in the morning. They said to leave the key in the car and leave the car unlocked. Nobody will take it."

"No doubt," I said. "Okay. Should we sleep here, or—"

"Goodness, no. We thought about Dad coming back in the van for you, but that didn't seem to make a lot of sense, not tonight. So instead, we've found a place for you to stay. Unfortunately, we were only able to locate one room."

"You found a hotel room for us?" I blurted. "Thanks, Mom!"

Of all the sentences I thought I'd say in my life? That wasn't one of them.

I felt like disappearing into my seat, falling through the semi-rusted floor. "I mean, uh, a place to, uh, take shelter from the storm."

"It's a room at a bed-and-breakfast," Mom explained. There was a slight pause, and then she added, "I know I don't need to say this, because we're talking about Spencer, and you, and I know nothing *would* happen. But you might check and see in the lobby if there's a cot available or a sofa. The proprietor of the B-and-B said the bed was a double, which is not very big at all. But in case something did happen—"

I pressed the phone as tightly as I could to my ear. I did not want Spencer to hear what my mother was proposing. I couldn't get out of the car because it was still pouring. Occasional lightning flashes lit up our faces.

"You and I have talked and I know you're practically an adult—okay, maybe you are an adult—but you're still my baby, and I know you know to take precautions and be careful—"

"Mom? *Mom.*" What *else* was she going to say? I didn't want to know.

I appreciated her concern, but this really wasn't the time to go over things, when I didn't have even a yard of privacy.

"Well, honey, these things do happen," she said.

"Yes, but not to me," I said. "Anyway—thanks for setting us up. I mean, for setting up everything for us. We'll go find the B-and-B." Maybe I didn't want to go away to college, because sometimes her taking care of everything was nice. Maybe she does micromanage, but at least she's good at it.

"Call me if anything—if you need anything—we can come pick you up, if you like," she offered.

"Don't be silly, Mom. Spencer and I will be fine. The weather's rotten, and it's late—we'll just stay put."

"Are you sure?" Spencer whispered to me.

I nodded. "We'll call you in the morning, Mom, but just assume that we're okay. Because we are."

I'm also nervous. Dying of anticipation. And freaking out. But okay.

Chapter 16

*W*hen the rain let up, Spencer and I ran most of the way to the B&B. Mom had given us exact directions from the parking area. I put my camera under my shirt to keep it dry, just in case the skies opened again. I was glad our clothes didn't get drenched, since we'd likely be sleeping in them.

At the bed-and-breakfast, this supersweet older couple named Mildred and Curt let us in, served us iced tea, and showed us to our room at the top of the third-floor stairs.

"Now, it is only a double bed, but it's a generously sized double bed," Mildred explained.

Spencer stood in the doorway, just staring at the overly flowered comforter, with matching curtains, borders, and floral prints on the wall. "It looks like a single bed," Spencer said.

Curt nodded. "You're right. Sorry, I forgot. This is our mother-in-law room."

"That's okay. I was going to sleep on the floor, anyway," Spencer said. "Don't worry about it."

"I'll go get some extra comforters—you can build yourself a little nest."

"What am I, a bird?" Spencer whispered to me as Mildred gave us a brief tour, showing us the tiny pink bathroom, and how the pink rotary phone worked, and where to find extra pink towels. We were both trying not to laugh, because the room couldn't have been more *not* our style, even with effort.

"You poor kids." Mildred patted my shoulder as they prepared to leave us for the night. "Well, I hope you don't mind that our inn is very romantical. I know you're just friends and this is a dire situation—"

"It's not dire at all, actually," I said. "We're pleased to be here. Thanks so much for finding a place for us on such short notice."

We said good night and closed the door. Spencer pressed his ear to it and listened for a second, as if he wanted to hear them go back downstairs.

"They don't strike me as the eavesdropping type," I said, wondering if my mom in her insanity had asked them to keep close tabs on the two of us.

"You never know," he said. "Is everyone else here already in bed? I mean, is this an inn or a retirement home?"

"What are you saying?"

"I'm saying, I feel like there are more vacant rooms than just this one. And our parents wanted to save money, so they booked us in the smallest room."

"If this is about sleeping on the floor, I'll do it," I said. "Because I don't mind."

"No, but do you want a picture of my nest? It's very romantical."

We both laughed. I went into the bathroom and brushed my teeth with my index finger—it was a trick I'd learned on our various camping trips over the years. Spencer did the same thing, then settled onto his nest on the floor beside the bed. I climbed into the bed and looked over at him. "So."

"So."

"Here we are," I said.

"Right." He suddenly got to his feet. "You know what? I need a book. I always read before bed."

"Didn't you bring one?"

"No."

"Wow. That has to be the first time in your life," I said.

"Ha-ha. I'll go get one from the lobby—they said they had a library."

I lay there and waited, nearly holding my breath. Then I ran into the tiny bathroom and scrubbed my teeth one more time with my finger, using the guest toothpaste. Just in case.

I was back in bed, under the covers in my T-shirt, just as Spencer came back into the room.

"You won't believe this, but all they have is horror novels," he said. "Oh, and cookbooks."

"Horror novels? Them?"

"I borrowed the one with the best blurbs. It's about eight hundred pages long. Oh, and here. Mildred baked cookies." He held out a napkin with a large ginger cookie on it.

"Cookies? At this time of night? Um, I just brushed my teeth." *For the second time. Because apparently I have delusions that I'm going to get close to you.*

"Oh. Well, more for me—"

"But I'm starving. Gimme."

"I thought you felt sick," Spencer said.

"That was hours ago."

"Yum. Cookies and a bloodbath novel. I'm going to sleep like a baby." He snuggled back under the covers.

"What time should we try to leave?" I asked.

"As soon as the sun's up."

"Yeah. Well, I guess it depends when Rustbucket sends someone to get the car fixed."

"True."

Did we really have this little to talk about?

"Are you going to be able to sleep if I keep this light on?" he asked.

"Oh, sure." I was trying very hard to be agreeable. But the truth was that the longer I lay there, listening to him flip the flimsy pages, the brighter the light seemed to get. I covered my face with the light—pink—cotton blanket. It smelled vaguely like gingerbread cookies.

Or maybe that was me.

I peeked over the edge and made sure Spencer was lying down focused on reading, then I got up and scooted into the bathroom to brush my teeth for the third time, and wash my face. When I came out, Spencer was lying on his back, and he looked up at me. Our eyes met and I did this kind of awkward move, pulling down my T-shirt. What was I doing, walking around with hardly any clothes on in front of Spencer? I scurried back into bed and under the blanket.

"You know what? There's too much pink in here. There's like a *glow* to the room. I can't read a scary book in the middle of this environment."

"You're so sensitive," I teased him, getting comfy in bed again.

"And *you're* so obsessed about brushing your teeth."

"I was getting a drink of water," I said.

"Well. Um, you can turn the light off now," Spencer said.

"Okay." I reached over and switched off the lamp on the nightstand. I rested my head on the pillow, lay back, and tried to relax. I couldn't, though. I kept thinking about how disappointed I was in myself, that I hadn't yet had the guts to tell Spencer how I felt. And if I was disappointed, Heather was going to be even more so. She'd helped create this opportunity. We were *alone*. We were in the dark. If there was ever a good time to tell him, it was now.

"Spencer?" I said softly. "Spencer?"

"Yeah?"

"Are you comfortable enough? Do you want another pillow?"

"I'm fine. I'll just use this book for a pillow. It's big enough," he said.

I laughed. "Um, okay. Are you sure?"

"I'm sure."

"Won't it give you really bad dreams?" I asked.

"Nah. Don't worry about it, I'm fine. I've

got this pillow from that chair over there, and it has a giant turkey on it. Very Thanksgiving. Wait a second. I'm hungry."

"Me too. Does the pillow smell like gingerbread, too? Because my blanket does," I said.

"Kind of. Do you think we're in a fairy tale? Like, which was the one with the creepy witch and the oven? That is so Mildred."

"'Hansel and Gretel.' Which one am I?" I asked. "I could never remember which was the girl."

"You're Rumpelstiltskin. No, wait—which was the one with the long hair? Rapunzel, Rapunzel, let down your hair."

I slid over to the edge of the bed and leaned back, letting my hair fall onto him.

"Ack!" he cried. "Don't scare me like that."

"Fine. I'll leave you alone. Quit reading horror novels and you won't be so on edge." I scooted back to the middle of the bed, put my head back on my pillow and lay there for another five minutes. He might be sleepy, but I wasn't. At all. I was keenly aware of how close he was, of how we could be talking, but weren't. How we could be kissing, but weren't. How this whole night was slipping through my fingers like beach sand.

"Spencer? Are you asleep?" I asked.

"Yes."

"Good. I want to talk to you about something," I began.

"Uh-oh. Is this going to be about me getting you another cookie?"

"No," I said.

"If you need help falling asleep, I can go grab a cookbook for you to read," he offered. "They must have *Best Gingerbread Recipes of All Time*."

"*No*. I want to talk about what happened the last time we all got together," I finally said, as emphatically as I could.

"You mean . . . the pizza party? When they forgot to deliver our pizza, and my dad insisted they—"

"No!" I interrupted. "You know what? Forget it." I turned over. "Good night."

"Yeah, okay. Good night to you, too." Spencer sounded a little hurt. I couldn't believe how difficult he was being.

A few minutes later, he got up and crouched on the edge of the bed. I turned back over and held my breath, wondering what he was up to.

"You know, when you said that stuff. Way back. Our last trip," he stammered. "I was a real jerk about it. I'm sorry. That's the reason I didn't stay in touch. I just felt bad."

"Well, yeah, me too," I said. "Obviously."

"I didn't know how to react, so I didn't say anything. That's not a good excuse, it's just . . ." He shrugged.

"I guess it must have been kind of a shock."

"Not really. I mean, I . . . we did have a lot in common and we . . . well, anyway."

"Right," I said like an idiot.

"Right. So, um, good night."

"Night." He slid off the bed, back into his nest of comforters on the floor.

A second later, I turned the light back on. Clearly, this could take me all night. "Sorry. But all the things I said back then. They're still true." I said. "I mean—"

"Can we talk about this tomorrow?"

Spencer asked, shielding his eyes from the light.

"Oh. Tomorrow. Sure. Fine." I switched off the lamp on the bedside table, turned over, and punched my pillow.

Then I sat up again. Cringing inside. It was like preparing to have one of my baby teeth pulled out, waiting for my dad to slam the door that was attached to the string that was attached to my tooth. But I couldn't cry, at least not yet.

"Actually, no. We can't. We have to talk now." *Oh, no. What am I doing? I'm going to be stuck out here—stranded—on an island that's haunted by a pirate's ghost, where I don't know a soul, unless of course Blackbeard had a soul, but actually I don't know him either, so . . .*

"Have to talk about what?" Spencer asked.

"Everything." I pulled off the cotton blanket, got out of bed, and sat beside Spencer, on the floor. "Would it maybe make more sense for us to both lie on the bed? It might be easier to sleep. And, uh, talk."

"No, I'm fine here," he insisted.

"Okay, but don't say I didn't ask." I hugged my knees to my chest. "Listen. I know this is weird. And we've known each other . . . forever. So it shouldn't be weird, but I actually think that's what makes it so weird."

He raised his eyebrows and sat up, leaning back against the bed. "Are you sure you shouldn't go to sleep?"

"Yes! Come on. You know how hard this is. It's like—you and that next-door girl. Megan. Magellan?"

"Morgan."

"Whatever. You couldn't tell her how you felt. And that's how it is with me. And with you, too, I think."

Spencer looked over at me. "You want to ask me to your prom?"

"Shut up. You are *not* making this easier."

"Should I?"

I stared at the little scar near his ear. I wanted to kiss it. I wanted to kiss him. "Yeah. You should."

"Okay, then." He reached for my hand, sending goose bumps up and down my arms.

"How about if I say something for a change?"

"Sounds good," I said, scooting a little closer.

"Here. Turkey pillow," he offered, and I propped it behind my back, smiling.

"Well, the first thing I have to know is . . . are you done trying to meet other guys on this trip? And if you're not—could you be?"

"Hmm. I'm not sure."

His eyes widened. "You're not sure? What do you mean, you're not sure?"

"Give me a good reason," I said.

"I don't think they're worthy. Wait. I know they're not," he said. "Blake and his cheesy jalapeño tattoo."

I smiled, remembering how he'd insulted Blake for me. "So what are you saying?" I asked. "That you *are* worthy?"

"Well, yeah, of course, but that wasn't the point."

"It wasn't?"

"No."

"It's okay, you know." I squeezed his hand. "You don't have to be creative about this."

"What, do you think I can't do it?" he replied, sounding offended. "Because I can be very creative with this sort of thing. At least . . . in my head."

"How about if I start by telling you . . . how I feel about things?" I asked. "I think that, uh, you're the Spencerest of all the Spencers I know." I'd told Heather that I'd never use that line, and here I was—stealing it. And it sounded just as stupid now as it had when she'd said it earlier in the day.

"How many Spencers do you know?" His forehead creased with worry.

"One. You."

"And that's a good thing?"

"It's a great thing. Only . . . you tend not to talk. At least, not about anything important. You read too much—"

"Well, you take too many pictures," he replied. "You never leave home without a camera of some kind."

"Well, you never leave home without a book—"

"Ha! What about today?" he asked.

"That was a fluke, but okay. Fine. So I'm obsessed. Get over it."

"No." Spencer shook his head. "Get over *here*."

We both moved closer to each other, so we were sitting face to face. I felt like my tummy was doing somersaults. Spencer reached for my hair, which had gotten all mussed up from the trip on the ferry, the rain, the constant struggling to get comfy. . . . He ran his fingers from my ear, down my neck, to my shoulder. I think I literally shivered.

"You can't be the Emiliest of the Emilies, because that's just wrong," he said. "And it sounds like a French movie. But you're . . . my favorite person. And I can't believe how when I saw you, I nearly fell over, because it hit me that I'd been totally trying to avoid feeling this way about you for the past few years since you said that to me. And I'm such a chicken. I couldn't say anything. It was killing me, but I couldn't do it. You weren't interested in me. You were interested in . . . Blake. Of all people."

"I wasn't, really—I was just trying to, you

know, have a fling, because Heather thought we should," I said. "I was upset when it didn't work out, but it didn't take me long to realize I wanted to be with you and not him, from the beginning. I was just trying to avoid it—and you. And this kind of, um, situation."

"What kind?"

I squirmed a little, feeling uncomfortable again, as if history was only bound to repeat itself here in a few seconds. "Where I tell you how I feel and you, uh, turn the other way."

"What? I didn't do anything as bad as *that*," Spencer said.

I nodded. "You did."

"Really? Wow. I don't remember it that way. I remember totally panicking, and thinking, we're leaving the next day and our parents are in the next room and what if something weird happens—"

"I thought all that stuff, too!" I said. "I just decided to take the chance."

"Yeah, well. You're young. You take chances when you're young."

"True. In fact, watch this." I moved closer

and kissed him quickly on the cheek, right by his small scar. Then I kissed his mouth, and it was nothing like the fast kiss Blake had given me in the grocery store—it was soft and gentle and kind of distracting me from my point. Then I nuzzled his neck, brushing my lips against the slight stubble he had now whenever he didn't shave. He was so grown-up. What am I saying? *I* was so grown-up. I'd never done anything so bold in my life.

"Some risks . . . are . . . worth . . . taking. I guess," he murmured, and then he started kissing me back.

Chapter 17

"*I*'ve never had gingerbread pancakes before. Those were awesome," Spencer commented as we walked to the car the next morning. "I kept thinking, with their love of cookbooks and slasher novels, maybe they're trying to lure us into some evil plot, but I don't care. Pass the syrup."

"I hear you," I said, but the truth was, I'd been too happy and excited to eat much of anything. I just sipped orange juice and played footsie with Spencer under the table. I was absentmindedly eating a cookie as we walked along the road—Mildred had insisted I take one with me.

We'd spent the night talking, kissing, talking, kissing, occasionally snuggling—I think I probably slept about two hours. When I woke up with Spencer next to me, at first it seemed like just another one of my la-la-land dreams.

Then he said, "Nice bed head," and I knew it was the real Spencer.

I contemplated snapping a quick photo— you know, just for evidence's sake. That seemed a little odd, though, so I kept my camera put away.

We'd gotten up around 9:00 and eaten breakfast with Mildred, Curt, and a dozen other guests at the B&B before heading back to the parking lot at around 10:30 to check on our car. I hadn't checked in with anyone at home yet and I kind of didn't want to. I liked being secluded, on our own "romantical" island.

There was a large, red piece of paper slipped under the car's windshield wipers.

RUSTBUCKET READY! it said. RUSTBUCKET TO THE RESCUE! HAS BEEN HERE. YOUR CAR IS GOOD TO GO!

"Why do I have a hard time believing that?" asked Spencer.

When I opened up the car door, another slip of paper fell out, which turned out to be the repair bill. SPARK PLUG WIRES REPLACED. MINIMUM EMERGENCY CHARGE APPLIED TO YOUR CREDIT CARD AS PER CONTRACT: $300. HAVE A NICE DAY!

So much for saving money by using a cut-rate car rental place. Living dangerously—or rather, frugally—could sometimes catch up with my dad. "Okay, you can be in charge of handing this to my dad when we get back," I said to Spencer.

"Get back?" he said, leaning against the car. "What do you mean? We're going back?"

I stood beside him and leaned against the car. The morning sun felt great on my face. But it reminded me that I didn't have sunscreen—or a hair brush—or anything. I was in desperate need of a shower. "I need clothes that haven't been rained on, slept in, and worn again. How about you?"

Spencer shook his head. "I'm fine like this."

I rolled my eyes at him. "You would be."

He took my arm and sort of twirled me

around to face him. "What? What's that supposed to mean?"

"You're so adaptable."

"Hey. I spent a lot of time the past six months sleeping on cots and other uncomfortable places, living out of a duffel of clothes and not always having a shower."

"I forgot. So, it's probably good I didn't see you then. Did you have a beard?"

"As a matter of fact—"

I held up my hand to stop him. "Don't tell me. I don't want to know."

"Well? Should we give the car a try?"

"I don't think we have a choice. Although now that it's daylight and not pouring, we at least have more choices than this," I said. I wasn't sure that was a good thing, after I said it. One great aspect to the previous night had been the fact that we were forced to share a space, unless one of us wanted to sleep in the car while the other slept in the B&B. . . . Well, *I* certainly wasn't about to volunteer for that. I wanted a room with a view. Of Spencer.

We got into the Rustbucket, where the key

was waiting in the ignition. "One advantage of a cheap car is the fact you can almost always leave the key in it. That may be the only one, though." Spencer laughed. He rolled down the passenger window, and before he knew what I was up to, I took a quick picture of him.

"Hey! What are you doing? You know I don't get photographed before ten in the morning."

"It's eleven." I took another one of him grinning at me, then slipped my camera into the little compartment between the front seats, leaned over, and kissed him.

"Maybe we should just hang out here today," he suggested after a minute of sitting in the car, kissing. "Do we actually have to go back?"

"Mmm. Probably," I whispered into his ear.

It was nearly impossible to pull myself away from him, but somehow I managed. I gazed at Spencer for another second as I prepared to start the car. He looked sort of uncomfortable and I didn't know why. "Are you okay?" I asked. "You look like you're getting a headache or something."

He rubbed his temples. "I can't find my sunglasses. I think I lost them in our room. Maybe they're under the bed or in the bed or something," Spencer said.

I laughed. "Well, that's embarrassing. You could go back and ask Mildred."

"I'd never do that. I'd ask Curt. But no, thanks, I'll just squint. Who knows, maybe they're here in the car somewhere?" he said. He began rummaging around the seat, looking underneath it.

The car started easily, and soon we were headed away from the shops, down the road toward the tip of the island and the ferry. I looked over at Spencer and said, "Remember. We'll always have Ocracoke."

"We will?"

"It's a saying." I shrugged.

"Not a good one," Spencer said.

You could make out with someone all you wanted, but you can't change him from occasionally being rude and arrogant.

* * *

We snuggled close to each other on the ferry, and when we got close to the landing on Cape Hatteras Island, Spencer and I walked down to the first floor and stood looking at the shore. I saw a few people frantically waving at the ferry.

We got closer and I noticed my dad's trademark green Linden sweatshirt. I saw Spencer's dad standing beside him, and Spencer's mom, and *my* mom. Did we really need such a welcoming committee? When I called my dad this morning to let him know which ferry we'd be on, I didn't expect him to round up the whole gang! "Well. Back to reality and parents," I said over the noise of the churning water as the ferry pulled closer to the landing.

Spencer suddenly moved away from me. I grabbed his hand, but he held it loosely, our fingers intertwined where no one could see them. "Let's keep this between us," he said.

"Really?" I said.

He looked at me as if that were an idiotic thing to question. "Really."

"Why?"

"Because everyone will talk about it, and us—"

"I can't tell anyone? Not even Heather?"

"Especially not Heather. Can you imagine the grief they'd give us? All of them? Our parents would be over the moon. Over all of Saturn's moons, too. I don't want them to interfere."

"But they'd be happy for us."

"Too happy."

"What's that supposed to mean? And since when can anyone be *too* happy?" I asked.

"Come on, we have to get into the car." He started walking away from me, edging through the cars on the first level toward the Rustbucket, which was parked midway back. We got in and I closed the door.

I knew what Spencer was getting at, but I still thought he was being overly cautious. "Okay, so you're saying we have to be secretive. Do we have a password? Do we have code names and everything for each other? How about . . . you be 'Curt,' and I'll be 'Mildred.'" I made air quotes. "We'll only meet after midnight under the cover of darkness—"

Spencer shook his head. "Forget it. I knew you'd be too immature about this."

"*Me?* What about you?" I shot back as the ramp lowered and we followed the line of cars off the ferry. "What's your problem? Why shouldn't people know?"

I acknowledged my parents with a quick wave and looked for a place to pull over, so we could meet up with them.

"What's there to know?" Spencer said. "It's not like we're going to stay . . . together. You'll just find some other guy, another Blake or an even dumber Neanderthal, right?"

I parked the car and turned to him. "Why are you saying that? You know that's not true." As I was looking at him, looking at that same face that I'd kissed the night before, that was now steely and arrogant, my eyes quickly filled with tears. I was glad I hadn't lost my sunglasses. I needed them.

"Hey, kids!" My dad pounded the top of the car. "We thought we should follow you home, make sure the car's working and you don't get stranded."

I got out of the car, not wanting to spend any more time in it with Spencer. My mom ran up to give me a hug, and I have to admit that I hugged her a little harder than I normally would have. She gave me a curious look as we separated. "You okay?"

I nodded. "Just tired. Didn't sleep very well."

"Who would have, under those circumstances? Was it completely awful? I hated sending you to a place sight unseen."

"The B-and-B was fine. Very pink," Spencer said as he walked around from the passenger side.

"And how was the rest of the trip?" his mother asked him.

"Oh, you know. Seen one lighthouse, you've seen 'em all," Spencer said in a bored tone.

I glared at him, wanting to kick him. He wouldn't make eye contact.

"So, should we follow you guys?" Mr. Flanagan asked.

"Actually, if it's okay, I'd rather ride with you," I said to my mom.

She looked concerned, but thrilled at the same time. "Oh. Well, sure. Spencer? You want—"

"I'll stick with the Rustbucket," he said quickly. "It's gotten us this far, right?"

"How about if the guys go in one car, and the girls in the other?" Mrs. Flanagan said.

I nodded, not really able to talk just then.

"Good call," said my dad. "Spencer, I'll drive, and you can regale me with tales of New Orleans."

"Okay, but no singing," Spencer was saying as they got into the car.

Normally I would have laughed at that, but I didn't find anything funny about Spencer at the moment. What was going on with him? He was the one who mocked me for having a fling . . . but what was ditching someone after one day? A *fling*, right?

Or, quite possibly, the biggest mistake I'd ever made.

Chapter 18

*W*hen we got back, I walked into the house and ran right up to my room, telling my parents I needed a nap. I'd never gone from utter happiness to complete misery in such a short time. There had to be a world record for this sort of thing. I didn't want the distinction of having it, but I felt like I must be close.

I turned on the radio, lay down on my bed, and clutched the pillow to my chest. Seconds later there was a knock at the door. *Maybe it's Spencer*, I thought, getting up to answer it. *Maybe he wants to apolo—*

"Emily? Let me in!" Heather called from the other side.

I opened the door and she burst in, quickly

giving me a little hug. "So? How did it go? I can't believe you were stuck there all night. How was it?"

"Horrible. And great. But then horrible," I said, and I started to cry.

"What happened? Oh, my God, don't cry. Please don't do that or *I'll* cry," she said. She grabbed a tissue from the box on the nightstand and handed it to me.

"You don't even know what happened," I said.

"Not yet, but if it's something to make you that upset, I can't handle it," she said.

We sat down on the bed and I told her about the fun night we'd had—and about the not-so-fun morning afterward, how everything had been great until we saw our parents, and Spencer freaked out about everyone knowing about us. "He didn't even want me to tell you," I said. "Which is so ridiculous. Like, how could I not tell you? And why?"

"Is he one of those intensely private people?" Heather wondered.

"No, he's one of those intensely insensitive

people. I mean, you don't have to tell the world, but you should be able to tell your best friend and your parents. You know? Then he called me immature because I made fun of him for wanting to be all secretive."

"But before all that—things were good? You told him how you felt . . . ?"

I nodded. "He said he felt the same way. I thought we really connected. I don't understand him. Why would he just—turn his back on me?"

"Because despite how cute and funny and great he can be, he can also be an arrogant idiot," said Heather. "Do you want me to talk to him for you? Or better yet, slug him for you? I have a mean right hook."

I smiled. "No. Not yet. Can I take a rain check, though?"

"You should just come out with me and Dean. Don't sit around here waiting for him to flip-flop again."

"Yeah. Maybe I will. How are things going with Dean?"

"You know what? I thought it was going to

be a fling. But it turns out we kind of . . . we really click." She smiled and leaned back on the bed. "It's getting kind of embarrassing how much I like him, especially since we're only here for one more week."

"Maybe you could stick around here the rest of the summer—get a job down here," I suggested.

"I thought about that. In fact, I've been thinking about it all the time. But can you imagine suggesting that to my mom?" She cringed.

"I know. You talk to Spencer and I'll face your mom," I said. "And if neither works out, you and I can spend the summer together somewhere else. Like Alaska. And then we can *not* go to Linden in the fall, because Spencer's going to be there and I won't want to see him—"

"No way—if we ditch Linden, we're going to California," Heather said.

I laughed. "You have this all planned, don't you?"

"And if things don't work with Spencer, he can leave Linden, not you," Heather said.

"There's no way I'm rooming with some total stranger."

Later in the afternoon, I was sitting on the beach, lazily clicking through pictures on my camera, when my mom came over to sit down next to me. "What's up?" she asked.

"Just looking. Deciding which ones to make prints of," I said.

"Can I see?" she asked.

"Not yet," I said. "I'll show you the good ones."

The reason I didn't really want her to see was that I was scrolling through all the photos of me, and Spencer, and me and Spencer. I'd gone from being so happy about having such great pictures, to wanting to delete all of them: Spencer and me on top of the Cape Hatteras Lighthouse, Spencer pointing to the B&B's sign, Spencer in the Rustbucket grinning at me. . . .

My mom turned out to be looking over my shoulder. "That Spencer, he's such a nice guy," she chimed in. "Always looking after Heather the way he does. How he stayed with you last night—"

I turned to look at her. "He had no choice, Mom."

"Sure he did. You both could have left or he could have left you there, the Rustbucket wasn't his car," she said. "He's a very responsible person."

I sighed. "Looks can be deceiving, Mom."

"What are you saying?" Now she was starting to look worried. "Nothing happened between you two. Right?"

"Right."

"But you're not hanging out," she observed. "I'd think you'd be hanging out together."

"Well. We're not," I said. "You know Spencer. He always wants to bury his nose in a book. Besides, everyone went their own way this afternoon. Heather's with Dean, Adam's at a batting cage with his dad and brothers—"

I stopped as I came to a photo of me and Spencer, one in which he had his arm draped around my shoulders, and we just looked right. I was about to delete it, when I stopped myself.

I remembered Spencer teasing me that day at Cape Hatteras, saying how I loved to delete. It was so incredible that we'd managed, finally, to get together. Why did Spencer have to go and ruin it?

"You know, I think I'm going to take off, too," I said.

"Really? Where? Do you want some company?" she asked.

"No, thanks," I said. "It's, um, something I'm working on. A secret."

"Really?"

"Don't get excited—it's just a camera thing." I stood up and brushed sand off the backs of my legs. I dropped my camera into my pocket and picked up my flip-flops.

"*Just?*" Mom called after me. "Honey, anything to do with you and pictures, I'm interested in!"

I glanced up for some reason and spotted Spencer standing on the deck upstairs in his usual place, holding a book, looking out at the water and pretending he hadn't seen me.

I just walked past without saying anything.

* * *

As the prints came out of the photo printer, I contemplated cutting Spencer's picture out of the group shots. Fortunately, the drugstore didn't leave a pair of scissors around. Or unfortunately. I wasn't quite sure.

They had a table to work on and even stocked the kind of calendars I wanted to use to give each family as an end-of-trip present. I knew we still had a week left, but I wanted to start early to give myself plenty of time.

I laid out the prints on the table, trying to match each one to a particular month. I flipped through the open calendar and stopped when I saw September. It was coming up much too quickly. I'd be at Linden then. What would life be like? Would I be anywhere near talking to Spencer at that point or would we just not make eye contact when we walked past each other on campus? Was it too late to apply to UW? I'd always loved the Bucky Badger mascot. . . .

I was lost in thought when someone came over to the table. "Nice pictures," said a male voice.

I looked up and saw Spencer peering at all my work spread out on the table. "Nice? Don't you mean 'immature'?"

"No, you—you really have a gift for this. The way you caught the light there . . . and the water . . ." He seemed to be fumbling for words. "Anyway. They're great. Can we, uh, talk?"

"I'm pretty busy getting all this together." I started collecting all my prints, wondering how quickly I could bolt. I didn't want to be around him.

"Em, look. I'm sorry," he said, stepping closer. "I'm *really* sorry."

I stayed focused on my work, as hard as it was right then. I just couldn't look at him. "I *really* don't care."

"What I said this morning—I mean, I was just—that was me being stupid. You're not immature, Emily. You're the opposite of immature." He tried to touch my arm, but I pulled away and shifted to the other side of the table to collect more prints.

"Now you make me sound like I'm ready for a nursing home," I said. "Which is it?"

"Be quiet—I mean, don't joke around, I'm trying to say something and you're not listening," Spencer pleaded.

"Oh. Wow. I've never heard of that happening," I said drily.

"You had the guts to say what I was supposed to say—and do. You're brave enough to face everyone with this and just deal with it. But—what if—what if it didn't work out with us?" Spencer asked in a quiet voice. "I just felt embarrassed. I'd told you so much. About dropping out and how I felt, and I—what if you change your mind? What if it doesn't work out?"

I finally managed to look up at him. "It's not like I wasn't taking that risk, too. And Spencer, we've known each other for so long. I think we both knew it was a good idea."

"*Was?*" he blurted.

"What's a good idea?"

I looked up and saw Spencer's parents, who seemed to have materialized out of nowhere. They came over to the table.

"They dropped me off then went next door

to shop," he explained under his breath. "Sorry. I didn't think they'd come back."

"Um." I coughed. "Making prints before my memory card gets full. Or erased. Or lost."

"Ah. What's taking you so long, Spencer?" Mr. Flanagan asked.

"I needed new sunglasses. I was, uh, asking Emily for her advice on picking out another pair, but then she started showing me her great photographs, and—"

"You lost *another* pair? That's two so far," commented Mr. Flanagan.

"I know, I know. I guess I, uh, dropped them," Spencer said. "On the ferry. I called, 'Shades overboard!' but nobody seemed to care."

"Emily, how are you after your overnight adventure?" asked Mrs. Flanagan, browsing the nearby shelves, while Spencer turned a rack of bumper stickers around and around.

"Fine. Just fine," I said, casting a glance at Spencer, wondering if visual death rays were just a myth.

"Can you believe how many bumper stickers

there are?" he said. "I mean, look at this." He held one out to me that had the standard abbreviation for Outer Banks, OBX, only on this sticker the *O* was the shape of two lips giving a lipstick kiss.

I raised my eyebrow. Interesting choice.

"What are you doing over here, Emily?" Spencer's father asked as his mother grabbed some items and headed for the register to checkout.

"Nothing. I mean, it's a surprise. Or at least it was." I laughed nervously.

Spencer's mom returned from the counter, while his dad went up front to buy some candy and chips. "Here, Emily." Mrs. Flanagan handed me a travel kit filled with tiny bottles of shampoo, conditioner, lotion, and shower gel. "Happy early birthday. Or late birthday. Whatever." She smiled.

"For me? Am I going somewhere?" I asked.

Spencer laughed. "Good one."

I glared at him. *Great. Now he's probably convinced his parents to leave early, just in case something else happens between us and he can't deal with that, either. Or wait. Maybe they're kicking ME off the island.*

"It's for when you get to Linden. You need your little kit in case you don't always spend the night in your dorm room," Mrs. Flanagan said as if that were the most natural thing in the world.

"Mom!" Spencer exclaimed. "Jeez."

"Oh." She giggled. "I didn't mean *that*. Emily's not that kind of . . . Anyway, all I meant was that she's going to take road trips with her friends, her roommates. You can have this kit and think of this great vacation whenever you use it. One whiff of that saltwater ocean lotion and you'll come right back here."

"Really," I murmured. *The question is: Will I want to?*

"Mom. You're hopeless," Spencer said.

"What?" She put her hand to her throat, adjusting a patterned scarf she was wearing.

"You're not selling the product, okay? You're buying it. You don't need to convince other people to use it," he argued.

Wow. He's even that rude to his mom, I thought.

"Well, excuse me for caring. I wasn't forcing anyone to do anything," she said.

"It's okay, Mrs. Flanagan. I really appreciate the gift—your thinking of me. I love little mini products like this."

"You do?" Spencer looked like he'd just lost all faith in the human race, like I'd committed a felony. "You're into products?"

I finished packing up my stuff. "Don't you have sunglasses to pick out?"

"Fine." He headed for the twirling sunglasses post.

"And don't get the same ones again!" I called after him. "Those were hideous."

His forehead creased with concern as he looked over his shoulder. "I thought you liked them."

"Yeah. I thought I did, too, but the longer you wore them . . . not so much." I turned and walked out of the drugstore, clutching my prints, calendars . . . and all-natural organic travel tote. That might come in handy when Heather and I left Linden for California.

Chapter 19

*T*he next morning, I was sipping coffee and eating a piece of cinnamon toast in the third-floor kitchen, where everyone tended to gather. Almost everyone was already up and accounted for, before Spencer wandered in and sat at the table across from me. He silently shook out a bowl of cereal and kept looking up at me, as if he was waiting for something. As if I would talk first, but why would I talk to him? I'd been avoiding him ever since the drugstore incident. I'd gone out with Heather and Dean the night before, just so I'd be out of the house—we'd gone to dinner and a movie, but the whole time I hadn't been able to stop thinking about Spencer.

So this was what really falling for someone

meant. It ruined your life.

I'd only bared my soul to him and what did I get in return? He told me I was immature.

Well, I wasn't.

Except that if he tried to say I was immature again, I'd say something in return like, "I know you are, but what am I?" which would only prove that I was in fact immature.

I had the potential to be immature, but I didn't exercise it. He did.

Adam came up the stairs in running shirt and shorts, carrying a bright red piece of something in his hand. "Excuse me, but what's this?" he asked the group.

"What is it?" his dad asked.

"I don't know — I just found it in the parking lot." He turned it over in his hand, and a piece of paper fell out onto the floor.

Spencer's eyebrows shot up. "I was trying to make a mini kite to sail, and that was the basket—" He leaped up from the table, nearly flattening Tyler, and tried to grab the paper off the floor.

Mr. Thompson got it first. He unrolled a

note that was attached by a piece of tape and a string to the small piece of red fabric. He read out loud:

"E,

You were right. I was wrong.

I guess maybe I'm falling in love. I've never been in love before. So what do I know what we're supposed to do?

But I don't care if everyone knows. You're worth the embarrassment.

You're the Emiliest of the Emilies. (Sorry.)
OBX XOXO,
S."

I felt my face get warm. Then my neck. Then my arms.

"Woo-hoo! This is hot stuff!" Mr. Thompson said, fanning himself with the note.

"Wait a second. Did that say 'Emily'? As in, this Emily?" Heather's mom asked.

"Who's writing you notes?" asked Adam.

"What does OBXXOXO mean?" asked Spencer's dad. "Is that some sort of code?"

"Are you getting secret messages?" my father asked, peering at me as if he suddenly didn't know me anymore.

I wanted to hear the note again. And again. Spencer was falling in love? With me? Had he actually confessed that? To a *crowd*?

"Wow. Must be left over from some other people. Must have blown down the beach," Spencer began. "Whole message-in-a-bottle-type thing —"

"Wait a second," Adam said. "Wait a second. S? Are you S?"

"Yes, Sherlock Holmes. You figured it out," Spencer said in a grumpy voice.

"Ha!" Adam laughed.

Spencer came back over to the table and crouched down beside me, putting his hands on my legs. "I thought I threw that little parachute onto your balcony last night, but I guess it blew off. So, I apologize for the public reading of my note."

"I don't mind," I said.

"Well, I do," Spencer grumbled. Then he smiled. "Yes, it was corny. Still, I mean every word of it. Even the dumb words."

I smiled at him. "So . . . you're okay with this?" I asked, as around us, everyone was murmuring and then shouting things like, *"You? And her?"* And *"Her? And him?"* and *"THEM?"*

"Yeah. I am. I'm more than okay," Spencer said. "I guess I was just in shock and I kind of overreacted. Maybe I ate too many weird gingerbread pancakes. I don't know, but I'm sorry—I acted like a jerk. You're right—this is a great idea."

"You guys! I can't believe it." Adam shook his head as he looked at us hug. "Dude. That's awesome."

"Well, I, for one, am not surprised at all." My mother smiled and looked very pleased with herself, as if she'd predicted it, which was ridiculous because even I didn't predict it. "Didn't I tell you? These things have a way of happening."

"Say something," Spencer urged me.

"Um . . ." I had no idea what I should say at a moment like this. It's one thing to have your first boyfriend and have him say he's falling for you. It's a whole other thing to have everyone in the world find out about it the same time that you do. And still another to have it be your parents and their friends. I leaned closer to Spencer and whispered in his ear, "Do you think we could go somewhere a little more . . . private?"

He nodded. "But you forgive me, right? You still think I . . . we . . ."

"Me and you? Oh, yeah. As long as you keep saying that you were wrong and I was right," I said.

"Don't get used to it," he shot back. Then we both laughed and hugged.

"Aren't they so cute?" said Spencer's mom. "They're so right for each other. How could we not have noticed?"

"Got bad news for you, Em. If your dad pays for the wedding, it's going to be an out-door event," Mr. Thompson teased. "Hot dogs, maybe. Generic chips and water. Not bottled water, either. Strictly from the tap."

"Give me a break, guys. What do you think I've been *saving* for all these years?" my dad cried. "Duh. She can have the wedding of her dreams. The in-laws, however, are going to be a major problem—"

"We're not getting married! Would everyone please shut up?" I said, getting to my feet.

But the guys were so busy arguing and laughing that they didn't even notice us slip away. Or so I thought.

"Hey! Where are you going?" Spencer's dad called after us as we headed for the deck outside.

"If you don't mind, we'd like to be alone," I said.

"Ooohhh, they want to be alone!" several of the guys repeated after me, in singsong voices.

My mother narrowed her eyes. "How alone?"

"See what I was saying? This is going to be awful," Spencer said as we closed the door behind us.

"Terrible," I agreed, taking his hand and squeezing it tightly.

We looked at each other and smiled.

"Somehow we'll just have to deal with it, I

guess," he said, slipping his arms around my waist. "In the meantime, we have one week left here, and I don't intend to waste it."

"Hey! You guys!" Heather shouted from down below by the pool. Dean was sitting next to her and they were drinking coffee together, snuggled on a chaise together. "Knock it off already!"

I waved down to her. "See, it won't be that bad," I said to Spencer as we stood by the deck railing. "Just occasionally mortifying. Come on, let's go tell Heather the good news."

"What good news?" asked Spencer as we headed inside and past the still-talking-about-us group in the kitchen.

"Don't make me—" I threatened as I stopped halfway down the stairs.

"Kidding!" Spencer cried, colliding into me. "I was kidding!" He grabbed my hands and pulled me closer toward him, kissing me. "You know, we have to stop meeting on stairs."

"Do we? I kind of like it," I said, kissing him back.

We ran outside and joined Dean and

Heather by the pool.

"You guys did it, didn't you?" asked Heather as Spencer and I sat down on the pool deck beside their chair, and put our feet in the water.

"Did what?"

"Made up! And went public!" Heather cried. She looked really happy and I couldn't wait to tell her about the note I'd managed to shove in my pocket when no one was looking. No way was I leaving that around for someone else to read *again*.

"We heard everything. The windows are open," Dean said. "We thought there was a fire or something, from how loud everyone was yelling. 'You, and him? You, and her?'"

"The 'rents are a little overexcited," Spencer said, nodding. "It's sickening."

"Or it would be sickening, if it weren't so great. Right?" I corrected him.

"Exactly." Spencer put his arm around my waist and scooted closer.

"Hey, if you guys want to be alone . . ." Heather teased.

"We're fine right where we are," I told her.

✳ ✳ ✳

A few nights later, our parents hosted yet another big party to celebrate all of us going to Linden. Mom had made a special cake, and a giant banner was strung across the deck that said: WELCOME LINDENITES!

"Do you feel like they had that banner made when we were two years old? And they've just been dying to use it?" Heather asked me.

"It does look a little dusty," I said. "And dated."

One afternoon, a large brown box had arrived, full of new Linden sweatshirts for all of us freshmen, plus two for the twins—Adam's stepmom had ordered them as soon as she found out Adam had gotten in. I took a group picture of everyone, including Dean, using the camera's self-timer and the TV stand as an impromptu tripod.

"Linden, my Linden . . . your tree is ever-lasting," my dad started to sing, in a deep—and deeply embarrassing—baritone.

"Sounds like 'O Christmas Tree' to me,"

Spencer said under his breath.

"I think it is," I agreed.

"You know what they say. Heard one school song, you've heard 'em all." He grinned, but seconds later an empty can of pop flew across the room and hit him in the head. "Who threw that?" he asked. "No, seriously. Who threw that?"

"So. We haven't really discussed this yet," I began as I started putting away the camera. "But what do we do when we actually get to school? Is it going to be too weird?"

Spencer looked at me and lifted a strand of my hair that had come loose when I pulled on my sweatshirt, pushing it back behind my ear. "Why would it be weird? I think it's great."

"You, Mr. Let's Keep This to Ourselves?"

"I'm over that," said Spencer. "Can't you tell? I've practically had my arm around you all day."

"True. And I love it, by the way," I said. "But what do I know about going to college and having a boyfriend? Nothing."

"Well, if you're still feeling weird about it,

why not take a year off and do whatever we want?"

I laughed. "Excuse me, but didn't you just *do* that?"

"Oh. Right." He smiled. "Yeah, but we could do it together."

As tempting as the offer was, I had goals I wasn't really ready to just toss aside. Plus, I could just imagine what my parents would have to say. "How about if we go be freshmen together, and sophomores and juniors and seniors, and graduate together? Then we can take a year off."

Spencer nodded. "Agreed. Except I'd like to skip the sophomore part, I hear that's a hard year."

"We'll go to Europe or something."

"Right. We'll do that, we'll *totally* do that."

I stepped back from him. "Are you mocking me? Again?"

"Would I ever mock you?" he asked. "Sorry. Okay, let's start small. What do you want to do tomorrow? Where should we go?"

"I don't know. Should we see what my mom

has planned?" I asked.

"No, definitely not." Spencer laughed. "I've seen enough lighthouses to last a lifetime."

"You're just afraid you'll have to climb all those steps again."

"Oh, *I'm* afraid? Really."

"Then again, if we ditch the group, like last time . . ."

"We're pretty good at not staying with the group, aren't we?" He held my hand, and I leaned against him.

"We can take off in the Rustbucket first thing in the morning."

Spencer kissed me. "If it starts, that is. Where should we go first?"

"I don't know, but we should probably avoid places with balconies," I said.

"And pink rooms—"

"And kayaks—"

"And family members," Spencer said as we spotted our moms sitting over on the corner of the deck, pretending to have a conversation, but spying on us.

"Okay, kids. Name the president of the

college during the tumultuous seventies!" Adam's dad cried.

Adam groaned. "You said this was a trivia test. Not an ancient history quiz."

"Oh! That's low! I think I need another beer," said his father, heading for the cooler. "Harsh."

"I thought they'd never end the quiz," I said. "Good job, Adam—way to appeal to their age."

"No problem. And by the way? Great cake."

"Thank you, Adam." My mother beamed at the compliment on her Linden leaf-shaped cake, which she'd worked on all afternoon. "You know, you can buy the pan at the campus bookstore."

Adam nodded at her with a serious expression. "I'll be sure to do that."

I covered my mouth, stifling a laugh.

Spencer turned to the parents. "So. Which one of you bribed the admissions office? I mean, what are the odds that we'd all get in? It's not as if Linden is easy to get into. Isn't the ratio something like six apps to one admission?"

"Eight, I think," said Mrs. Flanagan. "But the reason it worked here is because you're all very different, and you're all very interesting."

"Some more than others," I coughed, and Heather laughed.

"And that's what they want. Variety."

"So, maybe it helped that we were in your corner, and that we've given the school copious donations—" my dad added.

"And changed the world and brought glory to the Linden name along the way. Don't forget that," Spencer's dad chimed in.

"And instilled school spirit in our offspring," Adam's dad said.

"They could do this all night," said Spencer, scooting over closer to me.

"I know," I agreed.

"Do we have all night?" he asked.

I shook my head. "I don't think so. Actually, I think we're supposed to be somewhere. Right, Heather?"

She glanced at Dean and then back at me. "Yes, that's right. We're supposed to see, um, the beach. At night. You were going to get pictures."

"I was, wasn't I?" I took Spencer's hand and we edged toward the steps down to the beach.

"Come on, Adam!" Heather whispered, dragging him away from the Linden-fest.

We all ran down to the beach. As soon as we hit the hard sand, Heather turned and started doing back flips, springing down the beach doing one after another, just like she used to.

"Look out for the sand crabs!" Spencer called after her.

Heather stopped, waved at him, caught her breath, and then kept going, laughing and flying through the air. Dean followed along beside her, trying to walk on his hands, tipping over every other step.

"Hold on—wait for me!" I cried. I wasn't any good at back flips, but I knew how to do handsprings.

"Great. The tumbling twins are back," Spencer complained.

"I don't think they ever left. They were just in hiding," Adam said.

When I caught up with Heather, we hugged, laughing and out of breath. It was a nice feeling. So many things had changed, but so many hadn't, too.

I couldn't wait to head off to college with this group of friends.

And Spencer. Especially Spencer, I thought as he ran up to me and picked me up in an awkward hug, trying to twirl me over his head.

"What do you think? Is this ballet-like?" he asked.

"Not even close!" I shrieked as we both fell to the beach, arms and legs tangled.

"Sorry," he said, cleaning sand off of my arms, then my face. "You okay? Sorry." He brushed sand off of my mouth, his fingers lingering on my lips.

"Just kiss me already," I said, "and we'll call it good."

Read on for a sneak peek at

Save the Date

by Tamara Summers

I'm never having a wedding.

When I meet my dream boy—who will not be (a) boring, (b) obnoxiously fit, (c) an enormous role-playing dork, or (d) a Taiwanese model I barely know, like certain other people's husbands I could mention—my plan is to skip the whole inevitable wedding catastrophe. Instead we'll do it the old-fashioned way. I'll club him on the head, drag him off to Vegas, and marry him in a classy Elvis chapel, like our caveman ancestors would have wanted.

None of my five older sisters will have to be bridesmaids. They won't even have to come if they don't want to, except Sofia, who will be my maid of honor. And I won't force her to wear the most hideous dress I can find, because I, unlike most of my sisters, am a kind and thoughtful person with, I might add, a terrific sense of style.

Don't get me wrong; I love my sisters. I'm the baby of the family, so they've always taken care of me and treated me like their favorite toy when we were growing up. In fact, they were always super-nice to me, until they turned into brides. So despite the bridesmaid dresses they have forced me to wear and the weirdos they've married, I do love them.

It's just not safe to get married in this family, at least not if I, Jakarta Finnegan, bring a date to the wedding, which presumably I will to my own wedding. This is because the Finnegan family suffers from a terrible Wedding Curse, or at least I do. I don't know what we did to deserve it.

I didn't figure this out until after Wedding #2. I thought all the insanity at my oldest sister's wedding (#1) was normal behind-the-scenes craziness. When the best man got stuck in a snowstorm in Indiana—in JUNE—I was like, *Huh, weird*, and then when the organ player at the church came down with the mumps (in this century?), I thought it was strange, and sure, we were all a little freaked out by the flock of seagulls that crashed through the skylight in the reception hall during the cake cutting, but at no point did I think *Oops, my fault* or *Maybe I should uninvite Patrick to the wedding*. Afterwards, when this very first boyfriend I ever had broke up with me and fled in terror, it did cross my mind that maybe fourteen-year-old boys aren't cut out for nuptial ceremonies.

But it wasn't until the next wedding that alarm bells started to go off in my head. For instance, the day I asked my new boyfriend David to be my wedding date, the groom broke his wrist playing tennis and all three hundred invitations arrived back on our doorstep in a giant pile because they were missing two cents of postage. The day before the wedding, on the phone, was the first time I told David I loved him, and at that exact moment I got call waiting. When I switched over, it was one of my uncles hysterically calling to tell us that the hotel where all the guests were supposed to stay had burned down. And *then*, on the way to the wedding, when I kissed David in the limousine, *lightning* struck the car in front of us, causing a massive six-car pile-up in which no one was hurt, but everyone involved in the ceremony was an hour late.

Lightning. Mumps. And *seagulls*. I'm telling you, I'm not crazy. This is a very real curse. And that's not even getting into the emotional wreckage afterwards with David, but I don't like to talk about that.

So you can see why I'm not crazy about the idea of having a wedding myself. Besides, all the good ideas have been taken. There's nothing else I could possibly do that hasn't been done before. That's what happens when you have five older sisters.

But I should start at the beginning—Victoria's bridal shower, where it all started to fall apart.

Or maybe I should go back to Sydney's and Alexandria's weddings, so you get the big picture of what it's like to be a bridesmaid . . . over and over and over again.

Or maybe it goes back even farther than that, because to tell the truth, the trouble really started when my parents had Victoria and Paris only ten months apart.

Let's start with who I am (since I'm pretty sure that's not where anyone else would start). We'll get one thing out of the way right up front. My name is Jack. Under no circumstances will anyone call me Jakarta. It's not *my* fault that my parents are crazy and travel-obsessed, and none of us are going to encourage them by using my real name.

My parents are the Ken and Kathy of the Ken and Kathy's Travel Guide series. You must have seen the books—all about how to travel to fascinating places and have crazy adventures even with a pile of kids in tow. They travel all the time, always to exotic, fabulous, far-flung locales, and their house is full of wild foreign art and knickknacks. But it's one thing to hang an African mask on your wall or put down a Peruvian llama rug. It's another thing altogether to name your children after the cities you've traveled to, don't you think?

Mine is by far the worst, of course. I mean, it figures; I'm the youngest, with five older sisters, so they had obviously run out of decent names for girls by the time I came along. I think they were hoping I'd finally be a boy so they could get the Santiago they always wanted.

My sisters don't have it so bad: Alexandria, Sydney, Victoria, Paris, and Sofia. Those could totally be normal-person names, couldn't they? Not like Jakarta. I mean, seriously.

I guess it could be worse. My name could be Tlaquepaque, or Irkutsk, or Pyongyang. Or, you know, Pittsburgh. Sometimes I flip through the atlas just to remind myself of all the names that would be worse than mine.

That's me. Looking on the bright side.

Alexandria, the oldest, is twenty-eight now. She's a lawyer, and she's tall and thin and blond and perfect-looking all the time. Sofia and I seriously can't believe we're related to her. She got married two years ago, to another lawyer, Harvey the Boringest Man on Earth. That was the wedding with the snowstorm and the mumps and the seagulls. The one where Patrick broke up with me.

Then there's Sydney, who's a year and a half younger. She's athletic and short and full of energy, and she's a pediatrician. She married her tennis instructor a year ago. When I say "obnoxiously fit"? You have no idea. Marco makes me tired just looking at him. Even when he's sitting at our kitchen table reading the newspaper, you can tell he's burning major calories. Their wedding was the one where the hotel burned down and lightning hit a car and David was a majorly enormous jerk.

After Sydney came Victoria and Paris, only ten months apart and about as different as two people can be. Victoria, our "romantic" sister, is willowy and pale, wears her hair long and flowing like a nymph in a Pre-Raphaelite painting, and is very sweet and quiet . . . or, at least she was until she became a bride-to-be. Paris, on the other hand, has bright red hair cropped close to her head, a nose ring, and a burning desire to be the world's most famous female glassblower. My mom says she's "an individual."

Paris was enough to keep my parents busy

for four years. Personally, if I had a daughter like Paris, I wouldn't ever have sex again, just in case there was another one like her lurking in there. The world couldn't SURVIVE two Parises.

Luckily, what they got instead was Sofia, my twenty-year-old sister who is also my best friend and the biggest genius in the universe. She's graduating from college this year—she triple-majored and still finished in three years.

Then there's me. Recently turned seventeen. I have normal curly brown hair, shoulder-length, and normal gray eyes. I try not to make a fuss because I saw my parents endure Paris's wild teenage years and it didn't look like fun for anyone. By being a regular good kid, I get to do mostly whatever I want, and there's a lot less shouting. Also, it's hard to stand out when I'm with my sisters. If I tried to be loud (or naughty), Paris would be louder (and much, much naughtier). If I tried to be sweet, Vicky would be sweeter. If I tried to be bossy, Alex . . . well, you get the idea. So I try to stay under the radar, and I try to be helpful, because once Mom told me: "Jakarta, honey, we love that you're such an easy child," and that's probably the only thing that she's never said about my sisters—even Sofia, who was too gifted to be easy. (And you know what's nice about being the easy child? I'm the one they still take on their travel excursions. Not making a fuss has gotten me to India and Egypt and Paraguay and Portugal, so even when Paris gets all the attention, I still think I'm winning.)

I'm not blond or super-fit or perfect. Not romantic, not "an individual," and definitely not a genius. So what am I? I'll tell you what: a bridesmaid.

It feels like I've been a bridesmaid for three years straight, and we're not even halfway through my sisters yet. Victoria's wedding is this summer and then Paris . . . well, we'll get to that in a minute.

Read on for a sneak peek at

by Rachel Hawthorne

"I see a spectacular sunrise."

An icy shiver skittered up my spine, and the fine hairs on the nape of my neck prickled. I know my reaction seemed a little extreme, but . . .

When Jenna, Amber, and I walked into the psychic's shop, we didn't tell her our names. So Saraphina had no way of knowing my name is Dawn Delaney.

Sunrise . . . dawn? See what I mean? It was just a little too spooky. It didn't help that I thought I saw ghostly apparitions in the smoky spirals coming from the sharply scented incense that was smoldering around us.

Although I certainly didn't mind that the psychic considered me spectacular. If the sunrise she mentioned was really referring to me—and not the sun coming up over the Mississippi River. Her words were vague enough that they could apply to anything or nothing.

I'd never had a psychic reading before, so I wasn't quite sure how it all worked. I was excited about discovering what was going to happen, but also a little nervous. Did I really want to know what was in my future?

My hands rested on top of hers, our palms touching. Her eyes were closed. I'd expected a psychic to be hunched over and old—wrinkled, gray, maybe with warts. But Saraphina didn't look much older than we were. Her bright red hair was barely visible at the edges of her green turban. Her colorful bracelets jangled as she took a firmer grip on my hands and squeezed gently.

"I see a very messy place. Broken. Boards

and shingles and . . . things hidden," Saraphina said in a soft, dreamy voice that seemed to float around us.

Okay, her words calmed my racing heart a little. We were in New Orleans, after all. I didn't need a psychic to tell me that areas of it were still messy, even a few years after some major hurricanes had left their marks.

"I hear hammering," she continued. "You're trying to rebuild something. But be careful with the tools. You might get distracted and hurt yourself—more than hitting your thumb with a hammer. You could get very badly hurt. And worse, you could hurt others."

Not exactly what I wanted to hear. I wasn't even sure if I truly believed in the ability to see into the future, but I was intrigued by the possibility.

If you knew the future, should you accept it or try to change it?

"Lots of people are around," she said. "It's hot and dirty. There's a guy . . . a red and white baseball cap. The cap has a logo on it. Chiefs.

Kansas City Chiefs. I don't get a name, but he has a nice smile."

I released a breath I hadn't realized I was holding.

Then Amber had asked if she'd find love this summer. Since Saraphina's eyes were closed, Amber had winked at Jenna and me, because she has a boyfriend back home. She's been crazy in love with Chad ever since winter break when they first started going out.

Saraphina had said, "Not this summer."

Amber had rolled her eyes and mouthed, "See, I told you. Bullsh—"

"But college . . . one better than you already have," Saraphina finished.

That had been just a little too *woooo-woooo* and had pretty much shut Amber up.

Saraphina released my hands and opened her eyes.

"I see nothing else," she said.

Once we were outside, the heat pressed down on us. Until that moment, I hadn't realized how cold I was. My fingers were like ice. I shivered again and rubbed my hands up and down my bare arms.

"Well, that was certainly . . . interesting," I said.

As we walked along quietly, all of us thinking about the fortune teller's predictions, the aromas of chocolate and warm sugar wafted out of the bakery we were passing.

"Let's stop," Amber said. "Maybe a sugar rush will wipe out the worries about our future."

Once we were seated with our pastries, Jenna leaned forward, her blue eyes twinkling. "I've got a crazy idea. We should go to a voodoo shop and have a hex put on Drew and get a love potion for me."

"No thanks. I'm still freaked out about the psychic reading," Amber said. "I'm not sure if I'm ready for voodoo rituals."

The bakery door opened and three guys wearing sunglasses sauntered in. They looked a little older than us. College guys, probably. It looked like they hadn't shaved in a couple of days. Scruffy—but in a sexy kind of way.

They were wearing cargo shorts, Birkenstocks, and wrinkled T-shirts. They grinned at us as they walked by our table. The one in the middle had a really, really nice smile.

He was also wearing a red cap.

A red cap with a Kansas City Chiefs logo on it.